JARDINE

LEESA BOW

Jardine

LEESA BOW

ISBN 13: 237-0000520920

Editing by S.G. Thomas & Swish Design & Editing
Book design by Swish Design & Editing
Cover design by Najla Qamber Designs
Cover Image Copyright 2019
Second Edition

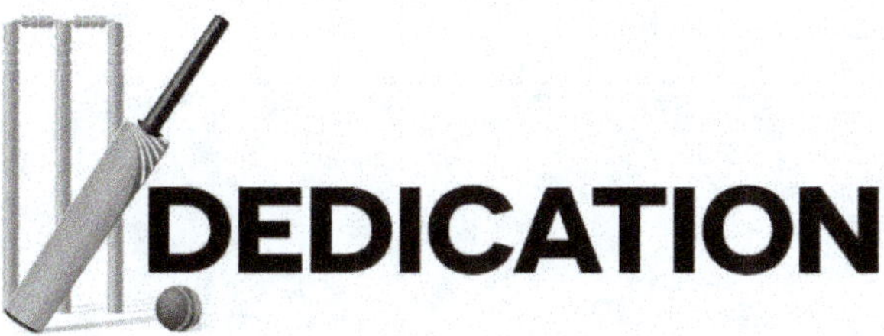

DEDICATION

To my family and friends,
who are the best cheerleaders.
Thank you for your inspiration.

CHAPTER 1

"What are you doing tomorrow?" Jardine whispered. He pushed a strand of hair behind my ear. His fingers lingered and slowly made a path to the back of my neck. I gazed into caramel eyes, slipping under a haze where only he and I existed.

My lips parted. His gaze fell to my mouth as though he clung to my every word. "Um," I managed before his head dipped. Warm, moist lips grazed over my mouth.

"You could watch me play cricket?" he murmured against my lips. I closed my eyes as he swept me away to *our* world, where the pressures of school exams and parental expectations didn't exist.

My hand skated the warm skin under his T-shirt. I groaned, finding solace, before he stiffened slightly, holding back. We were always holding back.

"I can't," I murmured, remembering my promise to Cleo, my best friend. "I have this thing..."

"What thing? Many of my upcoming games are interstate, so I was hoping—"

"I want to see you play but I promised Cleo. You know what she's like." His brow pinched. "I'm making a sacrifice to one of her deities. Yemaya," I confessed.

A smirk played on his curvy lips. "You're making an offering?" Being Hindu, Jardine believed in deities, but I was Catholic.

I nodded. "She thinks it will help with pre-exam jitters."

Jardine took my wrist and turned it, aligning my wrist with his. His finger trailed over the words of the tattoo on my skin, the same words inked across his wrist. "Visualise the words, Ava. Then visualise us and everything I've told you. I promise your school exams will be a breeze."

Ignoring the squawking seagulls flying over my head, I stared at the words *Que sera* inked across my wrist, and concentrated on the meaning.

It is what it is.

Focusing on the sound of the ocean, I closed my eyes and listened to the waves while breathing in the fresh sea air. I aimed to live my life according to my tattoo, the same tattoo I shared with my boyfriend. Yet it was my nature to worry, especially where my future was concerned.

Jardine had convinced me to get the tattoo a few months ago after I'd received a low score on my senior school mid-year exams.

On the morning of the test, Jardine had kissed my forehead and whispered, "What will be will be." I smiled back at him and tried to have faith like he did, but Jardine had a photogenic memory. I had to study triple the hours to get the same grade.

On that dreaded day, I'd opened the biology paper and my mind went blank. I panicked. Within minutes, sweat dotted my forehead and I stressed myself into a panic attack, unable to finish the paper.

Since getting the ink, I promised Jardine to look at my tattoo every day and repeat the words to myself in a silent mantra. He believed it to be therapeutic, and although it worked for him, I felt a little sceptic because for some reason luck or blessings didn't work that way for me.

Today, Cleo had her own idea as to how she could help me. I glanced down at the piece of paper and read the message I wrote late last night.

> *I surrender.*
> *I surrender my concerns of my present and my future relationships to the ocean.*
> *I surrender my concerns of my future studies and career to the ocean.*
> *I surrender my concerns of all my problems to you, Yemaya, great mother, and goddess of the ocean.*
> *I release all to you, divine one.*
> *I let it all go to you. I am yours to protect.*
> *I honour you.*
> *Amen.*
> *Ava.*
> *On the 7th day of October.*

After rolling the note into a scroll, Cleo handed me a small bunch of flowers and string. And not just any flowers. She informed me that Yemaya, the goddess of the ocean, preferred white flowers such as sea lavender. Yemaya also loved the fragrance of frangipani, or plumeria as she called it. Cleo had tied some in with the white lavender buds.

Did I believe in Yemaya?

I wanted to. Not only for Cleo but also for myself. I truly wanted to believe in a greater being—other than God—like my friends. It wasn't like I was replacing God. I was simply honouring a woman too.

Cleo believed that Yemaya was like the Catholic Church's Mary, also known as the Lady of Immaculate Conception. I was down with that part, but the whole fertility and patron of pregnant women thing...well, I didn't envisage needing her help in that department for years to come.

We were here for other reasons.

With my free hand, I tucked wisps of hair away from my eyes and into the elastic band securing my ponytail. I gazed out to the ocean, where my note would soon be sent as an offering.

"You ready, Ava?"

I glanced up at Cleo. Her tight black curls danced across her dark face, her brown eyes twinkling in excitement. She took my letter and flowers and secured them in a small wooden ornamental boat along with her note, then placed it on the sand. Cleo unzipped her backpack and pulled out a handful of pennies. She handed a few to me and placed three pennies under our notes before dropping the remainder back into the plastic bag.

"Pennies?"

"Mum brought them home from America when she last visited my grandparents." Pride filled her voice. "They're for good luck." I raised one eyebrow. "Yemaya likes copper and pennies," she added without looking at me. She then retrieved another bag from her backpack and placed quartz crystal, a few pearls that looked to be from a broken necklace, and a peacock feather into the boat. Finally, she sprinkled some small white seashells and tiny white flowers on top.

"We're ready," she announced.

My heart sped up slightly, which seemed weird. I had attended other offerings and I wasn't spooked back then. Although I'd always stood away from the group, keeping my distance in the sand dunes while I watched Cleo, her sister, Yasmine, and their friends perform the offering. But I never participated and never asked questions, fearing it was a sign of disrespect. The past twelve months Cleo and I had become best friends, and she'd suggested I do this with her to prepare us for whatever Yemaya had in store for our futures.

A future that scared the hell out of me.

On Friday we officially finished our last year of secondary school, and all that's left of the term was final exams—exams that determine whether or not I get into medical school.

Cleo suggested I offer all my worries and concerns to Yemaya, hoping she would take care of me. Apparently, Yemaya was very protective of her children.

"Let's go." Cleo wrapped the boat in plastic and placed it in her backpack before leading me along the sand toward the jetty.

"Do you think we picked a bad day? I mean the sea looks rough."

Something didn't sit right. Even on the southern coast of Australia the ocean was usually calmer than this in October. "Maybe Yemaya isn't ready for us today?" I scratched the eczema on my elbow, a habit when I felt anxious or nervous.

Cleo looked over her shoulder at me. She glanced at my hand itching my elbow. "Stop." She gave me one of her looks and my hand fell to my side. "The day is perfect. It's the seventh day of the month, so it must be today."

Oh yeah, that's another thing. The goddess liked the number seven, which was why I felt a little odd, trouncing along the beach so early in the morning wearing a skirt with six other skirts beneath it. Blue and white frilly skirts, because those were Yemaya's favourite colours.

I gazed at our long shadows as I walked along the wooden jetty, the sun sitting high enough to warm my back. We passed a few fishermen who each shot a confused look our way.

When we reached the end of the jetty, Cleo climbed over the railing and indicated for me to follow her down the wooden ladder. I wondered if it was too late to chicken out.

I leaned over as Cleo scrambled down to where the waves were crashing against the footings below. I noticed a small landing and Cleo waved me down.

After taking each step slowly, I made it to the landing without falling. Cleo handed me a large, conical seashell and then held up her hands toward the rough seas as though she had the power of Poseidon.

"Yemaya, goddess of the ocean and my dear mother, I honour you," she shouted to the wind. She glanced sideways then tipped her head, encouraging me to repeat her words.

"Yemaya, goddess of the ocean and my dear mother, I honour you," I repeated, although not as loud as Cleo. She then placed the shell to her ear, and I followed her lead.

"You talk to me in your song. I am here to honour you."

I repeated the words and placed the shell to my ear. Normally, I found the whistling sound of a shell delightful and always felt like a child hearing it for the first time. My breath caught when a shrill sound whistled from the shell. I gasped and turned to Cleo. Her calm expression indicated she didn't hear the shrieking coming from her shell. It lasted only a second before the wind tickled my senses again, but I swear I didn't imagine it. I inhaled a deep breath and smiled, telling myself not to take the offering seriously.

After a few more chants, Cleo kneeled and pushed the boat with our offerings onto the waves. Seconds later, the sea rolled over our little boat and swallowed it, sending it to the ocean floor. Cleo clapped her hands and turned to me.

Jardine

"Yemaya has accepted our offerings."

I looked up from my notes and into eyes flaming with desire.

"What?" I whispered.

Jardine closed his eyes slowly before opening them again. "I know we're supposed to be studying…"

I reached over to his hand resting in his lap. "We are, and I still have so many pages to get through."

He lifted his right hand from the keyboard and placed it gently over mine. I stared into his caramel eyes filled with lust. Jardine was my first love, and I was his. At eighteen, we were content with just each other, which didn't come without sarcasm from our friends. I pulled my hand away and traced along the length of him expanding in his chino pants. "This weekend will be special," I whispered.

His lips curled enough to confirm he shared my thoughts about the weekend. He leaned forward so his lips grazed my ear. "And I intend to make it special." My heart did a little flip and I blushed a little. Even though we had been together for a year and intimate the past six months, those special moments were stolen when our parents were out, both of us still finding our way.

In anticipation of this weekend, Jardine had booked a hotel room to celebrate the end of exams and our school life. Our parents accepted we'd be celebrating with our friends, who had every intention of partying all weekend, and I'd mentioned not to expect me home until Monday. The one thing I didn't mention to my parents was the hotel room I would be sharing with Jardine.

I walked out of the school hall feeling strangely numb. Somehow I'd managed to finish the exam paper and not freak out. I glanced down at the tattoo on my wrist.

I smiled. "Thank you, Jardine," I said quietly. His little pep talk before the exam had helped me, not to mention the fact that he'd left me alone last night so I could actually concentrate. Yet this feeling of emptiness and fulfilment together, the sensation of being lost and found, confused me. My schooling had finished and an unknown life awaited me. Like a fork in the road, the past crossed with the future to a whole new beginning. Destiny maybe. Yet part of me held onto the past and the present because they seemed safe.

"Ava, wait up."

Hearing Jardine's voice filled me with emotion. Gratitude, excitement, and lust to name a few. I turned to see students pouring from the hall doorway and spotted his dark hair first, his mocha-coloured skin standing out amongst the crowd. Some people cheered, some looked relieved, and others disappointed. As Jardine drew near, his expression blanked a moment as if trying to read mine.

"Hey." I flashed him an easy smile.

When he reached me, he wrapped an arm around my waist and led me to the side of the building. He cupped my face and kissed me, not caring who saw. With my free hand, I found the bare skin under his white shirt, kneading taut back muscles with my fingertips. He groaned into my mouth and my thoughts raced ahead to the weekend, forgetting all about the exam that finished merely minutes ago. He pulled away and kissed my forehead. "So?"

"So," I repeated and flashed him a goofy smile.

Jardine could read me like a book. "I'm so proud of you." His smile reached his eyes. "I knew you could do it. I've always believed in you. I just needed you to believe in you." He reached for my right hand, turned and aligned it with the inside of his wrist. The words that branded me connected me to Jardine far more than our matching tattoos. "It is what it is," he whispered for the fifth time today. His expression turned serious, and for a moment, I saw part of his father in him. "Don't think about the exam any more. We have only our future to plan. Forget the past."

I nodded, although I could not let go that easily. Yes, I finished the paper and thought it went okay. But whether the results, along with my other subject scores, were enough to get into university to study medicine, I didn't know. With Jardine's father a highly recognised orthopaedic surgeon, he was almost guaranteed entry. A wave of uneasiness ran through me, knowing things might change between us. Jardine narrowed his eyes at me as though reading my thoughts. Then he dipped his head and kissed me.

"One more photo," my father pleaded. I groaned and shot Cleo an apologetic look. "You ladies look beautiful. I can't let this special occasion slip by without a snapshot for our album."

"One's fine, Dad," I said, "but it's the eighth time." I loved my parents, although their way of showing adoration often embarrassed me in front of my friends.

Mum smiled warmly as she ushered dad away. "You girls enjoy yourself. Just be careful. I know you're eighteen, but..." she trailed off, looking a little sad.

"We'll be fine, Mum." I gave her a reassuring smile. "It's a big weekend. I'll text you, but I'll be celebrating with my friends at night and sleeping all day." Not a complete lie.

She nodded in acceptance but didn't seem convinced I was doing the *right* thing.

"Don't worry, Mrs Walters. I'll take care of Ava."

"That's what we're worried about," my dad shouted from the lounge.

Cleo giggled.

"Seriously," I said to Mum. "There are so many of us to look out for each other, and I promise not to drink too much."

"Thank you." She pulled me into her arms and planted a kiss on my cheek. "It's not like I don't want you to enjoy yourself, I just want you to be safe."

"I know." I hugged her before wriggling free. Passing the hallway mirror, I took a quick look of my black dress and make-up before following Cleo to her car.

We were only a block from my house when Cleo cranked up the music and bounced in her seat.

"Thanks again for covering for me."

Cleo shrugged. "It's cool. But you do have to spend some time with the girls and me. You're not spending every minute with him."

"I know." I turned and looked out the window and stared at nothing in particular. "I'm kinda nervous."

"What? Why?"

I turned back to Cleo. "I know we've done it before, but it will be different this weekend. It won't be rushed. We won't be expecting our parents to walk through the door any minute."

"I see. It's not just sex, is it?"

I shook my head. "No. I can't help feeling that tonight is monumental to our relationship. The beginning and the end rolled in together. I can't place this feeling, but it's weird."

Cleo shot me a confused look. "Well, us girls can fix your nerves. No hanging out with Jardine until eleven."

"Eleven will be pushing it."

"Let me deal with him. You're hanging with us girls 'til eleven," she said with finality.

We arrived at the party at eight and already people were falling over and spilling drinks. Callum Murphy, the sports captain, had rented the house months ago. There was no parental supervision; we were free to party—hard.

I weaved through bodies to the living room, where music blared and bodies grinded. I pushed my way onto a balcony overlooking the beach. The sun slowly sank toward the ocean, painting the sky orange. It was breathtaking. Cleo surprised me by placing a can of vodka and soda in my hand, and I turned to find her looking pleased with herself. She held up the can. "To finishing school."

We clinked cans. "To finishing school." I looked to the sunset, wishing I could enjoy it fully and not be haunted by negative thoughts about the future and the endless amount of 'what-ifs.' So much weighed on achieving a near-perfect score. It seemed impossible for someone like me...

Yet Jardine believed in me. If I failed, I'd feel more guilty about letting him down than the fact that I had let myself down.

I scanned the area, searching for Jardine. I pulled out my phone and checked the screen. No messages. Cleo handed me another can, urging me to drink faster. It didn't take long for the easy-going sensation to kick in.

Abigail and Chelsea joined us on the balcony. Both girls were blue-eyed, blond, tanned, and stunning. Cleo was naturally beautiful. Her dark skin glowed against her hot pink dress and ebony ringlets fell over her shoulders. I didn't stand out like my friends. I stood at medium height with long brown hair and hazel eyes. Basically, I looked similar to hundreds of other girls. Yet when my boyfriend looked at me with hooded eyes, I believed I was special.

After kissing the girls on the cheek, I glanced over to the group of jocks to check if Jardine had snuck in. "Let's dance," Chelsea said, pulling my attention away. She nodded toward the living room, where chairs had been pushed along the wall, making space for people to move freely to the music. I trailed behind my friends, not oblivious to the heads turning in their wake.

I downed the remainder of the can and closed my eyes, allowing the rhythm to control my body. I could lose myself to music. When I opened my eyes, I found that several guys had joined us, not surprising considering the way my friends danced. Oliver appeared in front of me, moving suggestively. I giggled and imitated his moves, moving my hips in sync with his.

Oliver and I had been friends since junior school. Before Jardine and I began dating, I'd sit with Oliver in class. Now, he kept his distance. He never openly said he disliked Jardine, but I could sense the tension just by the way they looked at one another.

Dancing with him, it reminded me of our primary school social dance. Innocent fun. Except the way we danced tonight reflected anything but innocence. Still, I felt carefree and it seemed harmless with Oliver. Chelsea moved between us, twerking her rear and making me laugh. I spun away and absentmindedly glanced at bystanders, my gaze locking with caramel eyes, pinning me to the spot.

For a moment, Jardine stared me down. Caught in his gaze, I forgot to breathe. Then he released me and walked away, out to the balcony. Instinct told me to follow, pulling me toward him like a magnet.

Leaning on the ledge, Jardine looked delicious dressed in dark jeans and a white shirt with the sleeves rolled up to the elbow, revealing his glorious skin. My gaze trailed down his broad shoulders to a muscle ticking in his forearm and beyond to where his clenched hands grabbed the railing.

"Hey," I said. "I've been waiting for you to arrive."

He didn't look at me. "Really. It didn't look that way to me."

"I was dancing with friends, waiting for you," I said in a quiet voice.

He glanced sideways at me. "You've been drinking."

"Yes, of course, aren't you? We're supposed to be celebrating."

"You know I can't because of cricket commitments. Besides, I have my own idea of celebrating." He turned and his gaze sent a clear message of his intention.

My heart fluttered. "Just have one drink with me to commemorate." I reached up and wrapped my arms around his neck and pulled him close. I kissed him and he kissed me back with a fierceness that shocked me, even with an alcohol-fuelled brain.

"Commemorate, you say," he said in a husky voice. "Fine. But not with alcohol." His lips curled upward.

Acrobats tumbled in my stomach. "So everything is set with the hotel?"

He nodded. "I'm driving so another reason not to drink."

"Okay. When do you want to leave?"

His gaze travelled down my body to my bare legs. "Now."

"We can't leave now. I promised my friends I'd stay a while. Remember, they're covering for us. We have the entire weekend."

He nodded, although it was clear he was distracted.

"What is it?" I rubbed his arm. He usually wasn't this uptight.

His head lowered, and my insides tightened. "It's not bad..." he started in a gentler voice, "I'm being considered for selection in the Australian team." He looked up and I saw uncertainty in his eyes.

"Hey, that's awesome, right?" I didn't know exactly what it meant, but my heart swelled at the possibility of him playing cricket for Australia. "You must be proud just to be considered?"

"I am. You know it's always been a dream of mine. But I never thought it would be happen...well, at least not until I was a few years older with more experience."

Three weeks ago, Jardine was selected to play cricket for South Australia. Last year, he'd shined as a junior playing against seniors in the domestic competition and his state selection at such a young age had placed him with the elite. I knew he would be traveling away some weekends to play but never thought he was good enough to play for Australia. Especially not at eighteen.

"Your parents must be thrilled." I rubbed his arm.

He nodded. "Dad is already planning to take days off in case I make the team."

Wow, his dad was a workaholic and didn't take vacation days for anything.

Jardine's grandfather, Sanjay Kumble, was one of India's best spin bowlers. Jardine had explained that the spin on the ball made it hard to predict, tricking the batsman into making a mistake because of the way the ball bounced. Spin bowlers didn't rely on speed but were more tactical in their approach whereas–Jardine was a pace bowler and relied on speed to get the batsman out. It seemed only natural for Jardine to follow in his family's footsteps, even though his father didn't play at a high level. Instead, his father had chosen to study medicine rather than throw himself into the game. After Jardine was born, his father's passion returned, and he'd even named Jardine after a famous English cricketer of the 1930's.

Hearing the news, I imagined his family celebrating. The hesitant look in his eyes troubled me.

"I am very proud of you." I snaked my arms around his middle and squeezed. He rested his chin on my head and hugged me back.

Then he kissed the top of my head. "Thank you. It might not mean anything, but I'm stoked that I'm being considered. Now go make your friends happy so we can leave."

"What are you going to do?"

He looked around the room. I followed his gaze to the jocks in the corner of the room, to Ewan. I didn't like Ewan. He was a footballer and thought he was beyond any girl. Already half a dozen girls surrounded him, laughing and acting drunk, hanging onto his every word.

I scanned the area for Cleo as we crossed the room to where the group congregated.

"Hey, man." Ewan greeted Jardine with a playful punch. "You want a beer?"

Jardine shook his head.

"Ava still got you by the balls?"

"Fuck off, Ewan."

My whole body tensed. "I'll see you later." I turned without giving Ewan any attention and set off to find Cleo. I'd never understood the "bromance" between guys.

My friends were downstairs in the backyard, hovering near the side fence. One of the guys standing near Cleo blew out smoke. When the haze wafted toward me, I knew it wasn't a cigarette.

"Here she is," Cleo announced. She stepped to me and looped an arm around my shoulder. Cleo knew how I felt about drugs, and I wasn't sure whether her possessive arm was to protect the guys or me. "You don't have a drink?" She feigned shock. "We need to fix that." She led me away and waved over her shoulder. "Catch you guys later."

"Not your type?" I mocked, knowing she'd just used me as cover.

She shook her head. "Nope. Let's fix you a drink and then we'll find Callum."

"So Callum is on your menu tonight?"

She laughed. "God, I do want to devour him."

We walked past the ice bucket and scooped up cans of vodka and soda. Cleo nodded toward Callum, who was standing with a group of guys that included Ewan.

I groaned.

"Play nice," Cleo warned.

As soon as Callum caught sight of us, he turned away from the group, smiling directly at Cleo. I understood her attraction to Callum with his broad shoulders and lean physique. He excelled at football and cricket, and along with his blond surfy locks, he was a catch.

"Ladies." He nodded.

Cleo clinked her can against his beer bottle. "Great house."

He pushed his hand down the side of his face. "Yeah, it's my aunt's. Gotta say I'm nervous about cleaning up tomorrow."

I gasped. "You're cleaning this mess up on your own?"

He gave me an easy smile. "I'm paying for cleaners, but I need to pick up the shit lying around first. Some of the guys are helping."

"I'll help," Cleo offered.

He looked at me. "Sorry. I'm with Jardine and we're staying in the city. I can chip in some money for the cleaners."

He waved a hand at me. "No worries, we've got it covered. Where's Jardine?"

Good question. "I thought he was here with you guys?"

"Yeah, but he took a phone call and disappeared a while back." He turned his attention to Cleo. "Dance?"

Cleo flashed me a questioning look.

"You go," I said reassuringly. "I need to find Jardine."

I waited for her to disappear into the crowd before turning to Ewan. "Have you seen Jardine?"

His dark eyes stared at me a moment too long before answering. "He's out front."

"Thanks." Not wanting to be near Ewan any longer than necessary, I headed toward the front door.

"Don't forget your whip on your way out."

I didn't turn around to give Ewan the satisfaction of thinking he'd gotten to me. I soon forgot about him when I stepped out on the deck. Jardine sat on a step, arms dangling over his knees and limply holding his phone in his hand, the screen still bright.

"Hi," I said, loud enough to alert him. I sat next to him and, without looking at me; he lifted an arm for me to snuggle under and pulled me into his side.

"Whom were you talking to?" I asked calmly.

"Dad." His gaze went to the street...to nothing.

"Is everything okay?" His expression told me otherwise, yet I needed to ask. I wrapped my arm around his middle and leaned my head against his chest.

He paused a moment before answering. "Yes." Then he turned and kissed the top of my head. "You want to get out of here?"

CHAPTER 3

I grabbed my overnight bag from Cleo's car before hopping into Jardine's white E320 Mercedes. The car was his mother's before she upgraded. Last year, my parents bought me a thirteen-year-old Corolla, and I thought *it* was special. I couldn't get my head around Jardine's parents giving him an expensive car at our age.

"What's the name of the hotel?"

Jardine smiled and then looked back to the road. "How about I keep it all a surprise?"

We reached Adelaide city central in ten minutes. Nightclub lights flashed onto the streets and Jardine slowed to avoid drunken walkers crossing without a care. We pulled into a bay of the glamorous Allure Hotel, and the concierge greeted us.

After paying the valet to park, Jardine hitched my bag over his shoulder and led me into a grand foyer. I tilted my head, admiring the décor of dozens of lights hanging from the ceiling. Plush red velvet lounges circled underneath and a suited man sat behind a piano in the corner. The sounds of classical music helped to momentarily ease my nerves. I followed Jardine into the elevator; disappointed we didn't stop and listen longer. He waved a card before pressing level 7.

My heart hadn't slowed since the car ride, and with each floor that passed, it picked up another notch. When the doors opened, Jardine took my hand and led me along the corridor, stopping outside room 707.

As soon as the door closed behind us, my bag hit the carpet and Jardine swept me into his arms. He kissed me, pushing our bodies against the wall. I inhaled the familiar scent of his minty breath from his favourite gum. His warm, full lips enticed mine and I moaned, falling under his spell.

Not so fast, my conscience warned. I broke away. "I need the bathroom," I whispered.

I grabbed my bag and took it with me. It was important to me not to rush things. I wanted tonight to be perfect. I cleaned my teeth, brushed my hair, and adjusted my bra and black dress. When I stepped out, the large, floor-to-ceiling window caught my eye. With the curtains open, the city lights twinkled before me. My gaze shifted to the bed. The covers were pulled back and Jardine was lying on the pillows with his arms behind his head, minus his shirt.

The sight of him took my breath away. Mocha skin gleamed and I could make out his six-pack. He jumped off the bed and strode to me. "Do you need anything to eat? A drink, maybe?"

"Some water would be good."

He opened the bar fridge and handed me a bottle of Evian. "Can I get you anything else?"

I shook my head after taking a sip. "No, I'm good." I strolled to the window and stared out into the night. "It's beautiful from up here."

Jardine stood beside me, our reflections in the glass blending in with the neon lights. His hand reached to my side and took my hand in his. I faced him and the passion in his eyes drilled into me. Large hands framed my face and then his head lowered, his mouth claiming mine. I opened to him, parting my lips, inviting his tongue to dance. When he finally broke away, he trailed feather kisses to my ear. I stretched my neck, inviting him to take more.

The zip to my dress opened behind me, and moments later I felt the material pooling around my feet. Jardine stepped back, holding my hand and guiding me to step out of the dress. In nothing but a bra and G-string, I stepped toward him. His gaze roamed over me, drinking me in, and I swear all oxygen was sucked through the vent and out of the room. I didn't move; neither did he. Sex before tonight had been rushed and we'd only been naked beneath the covers. Afterward, I would dress in a hurry, anxious of being caught by my parents. With no unexpected interruptions, I could relax tonight. Yet when his eyes lifted and met mine, every part of me tensed, stunned under his stare.

"You're beautiful."

I struggled to believe it, but then Jardine had his way of making me feel special. Then his gaze moved over my shoulder and his eyes hooded. I glanced behind and froze. My reflection startled me when I saw my bare cheeks in a black thong. When I turned back to Jardine, his lips parted. Without thinking, my gaze shot down and I held back a reaction on seeing his erection pushing against his jeans.

Seconds later, I was straddling him as he carried me to the bed. He lowered me and pulled my thong down my legs. I moved to the centre of the bed and Jardine followed, crawling toward me. With both his hands, he opened my thighs and dipped his head. And oh!

"Jardine," I gasped.

Another first for me.

Bunching the sheets with my fists, I opened my thighs wider and arched my back, moaning his name. A new energy filled my groin. With every lick, every suck, an unfamiliar sensation built in the depths of my stomach.

"Oh God," I moaned. I couldn't think straight as pleasure streamed through my body. Jardine's tongue continued to claim me, and just when I thought I could take no more, his thumb pressed against my clit. I felt a deep ache that climbed higher and higher until I came, colours exploding around me.

My whole body turned limp and I sunk into the mattress. When I opened my eyes, Jardine was staring between my legs, one finger skimming over my sensitive bits.

"What are you doing?" I murmured, still basking in the afterglow.

He glanced up and a cheeky smile spread across his face. "Getting to know you."

Jardine scrambled to my side and one finger trailed my cheek. I closed my legs, rolled onto my side, and smiled coyly at him.

"You're beautiful," he whispered.

My parents made me go to church with them every Sunday so guilt filled me after each time I'd had sex with Jardine. It had probably happened only half a dozen times, but each time weighed on my mind. "I just feel guilty," I admitted.

"Why? Because two people in love with each other are sharing that love? God promotes love, not war," he added.

I shrugged. "I can't help it."

"I'm going to spend the weekend teaching you not to feel guilty."

"Is that all you're going to teach me?"

His dark eyes hooded. "No." He rolled off the bed and disappeared into the bathroom.

Looking down at my feet still in heels, I grinned at my brazenness. I kicked them off and unclipped my bra, throwing it onto the floor along with my heels.

Lying in a luxurious room with a lock seemed like we had created our own universe where nothing else mattered and time was insignificant. I heard the sound of running water in the bathroom.

The door opened and my gaze shot to his naked body walking toward me, his semi-aroused package swaying freely. My heart thumped in my chest and I smiled. Jardine reminded me of a Calvin Klein model, only without the underwear and the fake tan. He was the real thing.

He stopped at the edge of the bed and ran his hand over his package. I stared. When he removed his hand, he had lengthened. I watched curiously, my eyes flicking from his face to his aroused dick. I didn't need experience to know Jardine was well endowed. The silence seemed to slow down time; the slightest movements made each second feel like ten. A shiver ran down my spine as nervousness and excitement flowed through me in equal measures.

He padded onto the bed near my feet, feather-kissing a trail to my knees. He climbed between my thighs and massaged in circular movements toward my hips, his gaze fixed on my legs where he touched. My skin tingled under his caress, the intimacy making me ultra-sensitive to his every touch. He kissed a line along my belly to my breasts and took my nipple into his mouth, his tongue circling the bud. I ran my fingers through his hair, watching his gentle assault on my body, feeling sexy and irresistible instead of guilty. He released my nipple and continued kissing up to my neck, grazing his teeth near my ear. He lowered his weight onto me, his erection pushing into my stomach. "You ready?"

I nodded. With one hand, he guided my legs apart, then he wedged between them. He lifted slowly and both our heads dipped as we watched him enter me. I gasped with the slight pain. Slowly, he withdrew before pushing himself deeper.

Jardine remained on his elbows, watching my face as he continued to fill me and withdraw in a steady rhythm. I tilted my hips as lust filled my body.

Staring into his eyes, I felt the connection and the adoration flowing between us. He pushed up onto his hands, changing the angle, and slammed into me harder and faster. Air caught in my lungs as a sharp pain shot between my legs. I closed my eyes until the pain subsided and pleasure built again.

His thrusts became faster, his gaze turned primal. "Jardine," I whispered just as I came. I groaned loudly, closing my eyes and enjoying sexual bliss. I heard him cry out and then he slumped over me, his weight pinning me down as he struggled to breathe.

We remained still and quiet, waiting for our breathing to slow. Jardine turned his head and kissed me. "My sundar."

My beautiful.

My eyes flashed open as a hand rubbed my rear. Sleeping on my stomach with my face toward the window, the curtains remained open and I knew it was still night. Early morning, maybe. Jardine prodded my hip.

"What time is it?" I murmured.

"Four," he replied in a husky voice.

I turned my head, my breath catching when the city lights highlighted his darkened eyes. "Have you even slept?" I croaked.

"No."

Then a finger entered me and I lifted my rear, groaning. It felt good, but I was sore...and tired, and yet I was wet and ready.

"Jardine —"

Jardine climbed onto my back, pushed my thighs apart and slid into me. "You're so wet for me." His lips grazed my ear. "You drive me crazy, baby."

I loved that I could do that to him, that he found me irresistible. I opened my legs wider, encouraging him. We'd never had sex this way and I quickly found my bliss. Jardine was right. I was slick and ready, my body quick to respond to his.

One hand reached under my stomach and he lifted me onto all fours. I called out when Jardine held me by the hips and pumped himself into me. Ecstasy built between my thighs. With one hand, he reached around and rubbed my clit. It was enough to send me toppling over the cliff. I cried out loud this time, exhilarated and exhausted, swollen and sated, I collapsed onto the bed. But Jardine didn't stop. I could hear his breathing change as he rode me into the sheets. He groaned something in Hindi and fell on top of me, his warm breath blowing in my ear.

In perfect timing, the sun broke through the surrounding buildings, light streaming through the window. He rolled off me and pulled me into his arms. Lying on our sides, he looked into my eyes and held my gaze. "I love you, Ava."

My heart fluttered. "I love you too," I murmured.

His face lit up even with his slight smile. "You're my world. You know that, right?" he said, and kissed my nose.

I cupped his face and nodded. Even though I liked hearing him say the words, his eyes told me all I needed to know. "And you mean everything to me."

"If you don't wake, we'll miss breakfast."

I forced my eyes open. "You go and bring back some fruit," I mumbled. No way I could get up yet.

Jardine chuckled. He sat next to me, dressed in a grey T-shirt and a pair of jeans. Based on the delicious scent wafting over me, I could tell he'd showered already.

He smiled knowingly. "You shower and I'll bring you back some food. I'm thinking you could use some private time."

"What've you got planned today?" Surely he didn't want more sex?

"I have a cricket game and need to leave at midday. You can come with me or wait here, it's up to you."

Hell, I forgot. "Would you care if I stay? I might wander down to the mall for a while."

Jardine held a straight face before giving me a nod. "Sure. I'll be back soon with breakfast."

As soon as the door closed behind him, I jumped up and slipped into a robe. Lying around naked had felt liberating, but now that the alcohol had worn off and I was alone, awkwardness crept in. I unplugged my phone from the charger and called Cleo.

"Hey," she answered. "A good night?"

"Yeah. You?"

"Yeah. I stayed at the house with Callum. I can't talk now. He's just in the other room."

"Is he as hot as everyone says he is?" I said, teasing her.

"Hotter," she said in a quiet voice.

I laughed. "So what time are you leaving there?"

"He's asked me out tonight. Can you believe that?"

I sighed loudly. "I'm happy for you."

"Perhaps we could all meet up later?"

"I can't. Jardine is playing cricket and since we're staying in the city, I'm going to hang at the mall."

"You're not going to watch him?" Her voice picked up a notch.

"You think I should? It's not like I'll know anyone to sit with."

"Yeah, I think you should. He would like you supporting him by being there. You know how he is with that sort of thing."

I nodded. "Yeah, I do. Mum hasn't called you?"

"No. Relax, Ava. She's not going to check up on you when she thinks you're with me."

"Can I ask you something?" I massaged the back of my neck.

"Sure."

"I knew Jardine and I were going to have sex, but," I paused, "is it normal to have like a lot of sex and the guy still wants more?" My cheeks heated when Jardine walked through the door, hearing my last sentence.

"Yes, Ava, it's normal. You two might not get a chance again for a while. You should be using this time to your advantage to figure out what you like and where you like to be touched."

"Aha," I whispered. My eyes locked with Jardine's as he stalked toward me.

"He's there, isn't he?"

"Yeah."

"He loves you, Ava. Don't be afraid to let yourself go. Be with him, like *really* be with him. Share your soul, because I'm pretty sure he's willing to give you his."

"I'll call you later."

I placed my phone on the bedside table as Jardine sat next to me on the bed, spreading fruit and tubs of yogurt across the sheets.

"I'm curious," he said. "Is my sexual appetite normal, according to Cleo?"

I peeled a banana, thinking about Cleo's advice.

Let go.

He studied my expression, waiting for me to answer. I slipped the banana into my mouth, curling my lips around it. Jardine's eyes narrowed. I pulled it out and licked the tip. "Apparently, yes." I sucked the banana back between my lips, my gaze locking with his.

"Are you deliberately making me crazy?"

"Maybe. Do I make you crazy?"

Jardine closed his eyes. A moment later, he opened them. "Ava." His voice sounded husky. He removed the banana from my mouth and took a bite before handing it back to me. "I'm not sure how I fell so hard, but I don't care what happens in my life as long as I have you."

Whoa. When did we go from playful to serious?

He picked up my hand, the warmth enveloping my skin. "I don't care what my friends say or what our parents think. I know we're young, but you're all I care about."

My gaze flicked over his face. "Come on, Jardine," I said in a joking tone. "You care about becoming a doctor. Are you seriously telling me you wouldn't care if you didn't get into med school?"

He shook his head. "If it meant losing you, then no."

My chest tightened, thinking about his father's reaction if I ever got in the way of his son's career.

"What about cricket? If you play for Australia, we might have to be apart…" And for months, I assumed.

"Then I'd turn them down, if that's what you wanted."

"Jardine," I breathed. "You've supported me through stressful times and urged me to follow my dreams. What sort of person would I be if I stopped you from following yours?"

"Nothing is worth losing you," he whispered.

"You wouldn't lose me. I would be there to support you and help you reach your dreams." I smiled and ran my hand down his gorgeous face. "So today I'd like to go to your game and watch you play."

Jardine's face lit up. He studied me a moment and then he winked, showing his more playful side. "Then I'll bring out my best game for you."

CHAPTER
4

Cricket didn't excite me.

However, watching my boyfriend run toward the pitch and bowl a ball at lightning speed toward the batsman somehow turned me on.

Over the winter months, Jardine had worked hard in the gym, developing strong shoulders and upper back muscles to improve his bowling. Evidently, it had paid off. And watching him today, taking four wickets in two hours, I understood why the Australian selectors wanted him. He was the youngest cricket player on his team by two years, although his age didn't dictate his height. Jardine towered over many of the senior players. Soon, he could be the youngest Australian player. I didn't want to think about that. Deep down, I hoped the selectors overlooked him, deciding that he was too young to make the team.

My chin dipped.

Selfish.

Yet after his performance today, even I'd select him. Maybe it was me? Maybe the sex spurred him on? Memories of last night flashed through my head and my insides tingled.

Jardine sprinted to the crease and leapt into the air, then hurled the ball toward the wicket. The batsman blocked the ball and by his awkward posture, it looked like Jardine had gotten the better of him.

After Jardine bowled his six attempts, his 'over' finished, another bowler replaced him. It was the first time I'd ever counted because, until today, I didn't know there were six bowls in an over, along with some of the other rules Jardine had explained to me in the car. My stomach fluttered remembering his expression as he explained cricket terms. Only Jardine could make the game sound exciting and sexy, especially with his hand inching higher on my thigh.

I straightened in my seat as Jardine walked to the outer part of the oval and directly toward me. Earlier today, I'd found a seat away from the crowd on the wing of the stands, only a dozen rows from the fence.

He walked with his head down as though deep in thought. Just before the boundary, Jardine glanced up, his gaze travelling over the crowd until he found me. I smiled and gave him a little wave.

His lips curled up slightly before he turned away, concentrating again on the game. While Jardine had a rest from bowling, I took the opportunity to find something to eat, considering all I'd eaten was fruit and yogurt for breakfast.

I headed behind the stands to a grassy area lined with brass statues of famous cricket players. I stopped to read each name on a plaque, but the only name I recognised was Sir Donald Bradman.

Food vans were parked in a semi-circle around the edge of the grass. I strolled silently, weighing my options between gourmet hotdogs, fries, pies and pasties, or Indian. I contemplated Indian, then thought better of it. Jardine's grandfather had passed down a family recipe for Butter Chicken and I doubted the food here measured up to his. I decided on fries, remembering Jardine had mentioned dining out for dinner and not wanting to spoil my appetite.

After paying for the fries, I wandered back toward the stands, thinking about Jardine taking me somewhere romantic. Usually, money didn't impress me, but damn I enjoyed him spoiling me this weekend.

"Ava?"

I stilled at the sound of my name, recognising the deep voice. I turned to find Jardine's father, Ajay Kumble, towering behind me, dressed in a black suit, white shirt, and a red tie. Jardine had inherited his good looks and his height.

His gaze roamed over me. Internally, I shrank away; feeling underdressed in my skirt, white top, and sandals.

"I'm surprised to see you. Is this your first time?"

His sarcastic tone didn't go unnoticed. "Yes." I only went to Jardine's cricket school games before.

"Hmm, I see. He's bowling magnificently. His grandfather would be proud."

"Yes," I said again, and managed a smile. At least I knew the history behind his famous grandfather.

"Well, my son has picked the perfect time to shine. The scouts are here and will feed his performance back to the selectors." He eyed me carefully. "Jardine will more than likely be selected for the Australian team."

More than likely?

"He mentioned being under consideration, but he doesn't believe he'll be selected." I struggled to keep my voice even.

Mrs Kumble made a noise like a laugh and a cough together. "Dear girl, Jardine is somewhat modest. I informed him on the phone last night how serious the coaches are about selecting him. I also stressed my concern about him *partying*." He sounded unimpressed just saying the word. "He assures me it's merely a procedure of final school year formalities. He has no intention of drinking and ruining any chance of making the Australian team. I hope you're not encouraging him?"

"Of course not. I'd never do anything to jeopardise his future. I know his dream is to play for Australia. I just didn't expect it to happen so soon." With each word, emotion swelled inside of me.

"Many people underestimated my son's potential. He's quite unique and thankfully has been rewarded for his hard work and dedication at a young age. Not many boys get an opportunity like this. He mustn't blow his chances with stupidity."

I nodded yet cringed at the way he said 'stupidity.' I also noticed how he called Jardine a boy, implying that he wasn't capable of making important decisions.

"I know you two have become close friends, but... he will be moving on with his life. I hope he's explained that to you?" His brow creased as he waited for my answer.

It would have been less painful if he'd punched me in the stomach. I sucked in a deep breath and tried to appear composed. I swallowed the lump in my throat, feeling disappointment claw at me from hearing this from Mr Kumble and not Jardine. "Yes, sir." My fingers played with the material of my skirt. I looked away and then to the ground, anywhere to escape his interrogation.

"Well, I must get back to the other gentlemen."

I looked up and thought I saw a smirk on his lips. Surely he wasn't that mean to enjoy watching me crumble?

Mr Kumble patted his tie. "Oh, and good luck with your results...in case I don't see you."

What? My school results were not due for another eight weeks.

"What is it you intend to study?" He raised one eyebrow.

Jardine had very few personality characteristics of his father. Because Mr Kumble worked as an orthopaedic surgeon, he'd often work late, so I'd missed him at the few dinners that his mother had invited me to attend. I decided I didn't like him and was thankful that I hadn't seen him on those occasions.

Yet his behaviour seemed odd, and I wondered if he thought of me as a threat to his son's future. If so, his weakness shifted the power to me.

This time I held my head high. "Jardine convinced me to study medicine and apply to the same university as him. We've been planning it a while and sent our applications off together."

"Did you sit the UMAT?"

"Yes, and I received a satisfactory score."

His hand went to the back of his neck. "Jardine didn't consult with me about his university application. There are other universities in Australia he should consider. As his friend, I'd appreciate you encouraging him to apply where *I* think best suits him. At the moment, the University of Sydney is preferable. Do you mind having a word with my son?"

I smiled like the Cheshire cat. "Of course. Although I expect Jardine will decide what's best for himself, regardless of what I say."

"And I expect him not to be influenced by your ideas as well, Ava. Unless, of course, they mirror mine. Enjoy the game and please do not entice my son to partake in any silly behaviour over the weekend."

"We intend on having a quiet night and going out to dinner." I watched him digest my words, hoping he knew Jardine was spending the night with me. Part of me wanted to compete with him for Jardine's affection, but then I thought better of it.

He nodded and walked away. At first, I felt slightly triumphant...until the previous conversation repeated in my mind and the reality of his words hit me with the force of a cricket bat. Jardine might be selected for the Australian team, and while living away from home, he'd move on with his life —without me.

I no longer wanted the bucket of fries in my hand. I walked over to the trashcan and dumped the fries before slipping into the restroom to take control of my emotions.

Jardine

"You're quiet," Jardine said as we drove to his favourite Italian restaurant. "In fact, you've been quiet ever since the game. Something up?"

I shrugged. "No. Just tired. Lack of sleep." I grinned at him. As much as I wanted to tell Jardine about his dad, there was no way of blurting it out without sounding infantile.

Hey, I don't like your dad. He's really mean. I cringed. *Your dad thinks I'm not good enough for you!*

Jardine might react and challenge his father. The last thing I wanted was to cause problems in his family and get on his parents' bad side. So I decided not to mention the conversation with his father.

After being seated inside the Italian restaurant at an intimate table for two, Jardine ordered water for himself and a bottle of sparkling wine for me. I raised one eyebrow at him. When the waiter walked away, I lifted my foot and touched his knee. "You know I'm a cheap drunk. One glass and I'm anyone's," I joked.

Jardine's brow furrowed. "Not. Anyone's. Ava." He leaned forward so only I could hear him. "Never think you're anyone's or ever will be. I thought I made that clear last night."

Our gazes locked, his caramel eyes penetrating mine. I held my breath and rubbed my foot along his thigh. "You did. I'm joking, babe." His shoulders relaxed and his hands wrapped around my ankle, gently massaging the skin.

"You don't need to drink the whole bottle. I want to pamper you tonight, give you what you want."

"I don't need pampering. I only need you." I tilted my head. "I thought I made that clear last night."

His fingers made little circles on my ankle, sending tingles along my leg. "You did. But I'm feeling happy and want to give my girlfriend some special treatment. Is that okay?"

I nodded. "You should be happy. You played a good game. If the selectors were there today, they'd pick you for sure." I smiled innocently.

Jardine's gaze lowered. He released my ankle and one of his hands grabbed the fork, twirling it in his fingers. "The selectors were there today and I heard they were impressed with my game."

"That's awesome." I feigned happiness, but my voice sounded a little too high even to my own ears. I concentrated on controlling my tone. "I'm very proud of you. You deserve to be selected, Jardine. You've worked hard and it's your dream." I smiled reassuringly. "You should call your friends and we can celebrate tonight. Have a party in our room."

He shot me a confused look. "Nothing is set, Ava. Besides, I don't want to celebrate with them. I want to spend the night with you."

His father sounded more convinced about him making the team, and yet I couldn't reveal our little conversation. "Well, let's order our meal so we can go celebrate…together."

"Hello, Jardine," a sweet voice interrupted.

Out of reflex, I removed my foot from his thigh. I glanced up to see a middle-aged lady dressed in a grey tailored skirt, white blouse, and grey jacket. Her dark hair was pulled high into a bun on the top of her head.

"Michelle. It's nice to see you." Jardine stood and hugged the lady, then remained standing by her side. Her gaze flicked from Jardine to me. "This is my girlfriend, Ava. Ava, Michelle. Dad's nurse who works in his medical practice."

I stood when Michelle offered her hand, and shook it. "Nice to meet you, Michelle." I tugged at the hem of my black dress, the same dress I wore to the party the night before.

"Your father never mentioned you having a girlfriend." She looked at me curiously.

My hand involuntarily went to my elbow. "Really? We've been together for a year."

Jardine gaped at me. Internally, I cringed. I hadn't meant to blurt that out. Why did I sound defensive? Our relationship was none of his father's business.

"I see," she said and smiled. "Might've slipped his mind."

"Well, thank you for stopping and saying hello," Jardine added quickly.

Michelle flashed a wry smile. "You young lovebirds enjoy your dinner." She kissed Jardine on the cheek before heading to her table.

Young lovebirds.

Why did people not take our love seriously?

"Why do you think your father hasn't mentioned me?"

Jardine's expression remained blank. "You know my father. His life is all work or cricket."

"He doesn't like me," I murmured.

"Why would you think that? My father would hardly talk about my love life at his workplace."

I nodded. I held my tongue; afraid I might let more slip. The waiter appeared and poured the sparkling wine into my glass. He waited for me to taste the wine and give him the nod. I did and after he filled my glass, I downed the wine in one swift action. I held up the glass and the waiter refilled the crystal flute.

Jardine didn't comment. Instead, he turned to the waiter and asked him to take our meal order. For the remainder of the night, our conversation remained stilted with comments made regarding the food or the black and red décor of the restaurant.

At the end of the evening, Jardine took my hand as we walked back to his car. He walked me to the passenger side, opened the door, and closed it behind me. I watched him stride around the front of the car. As soon as he was seated, he twisted to face me.

"You're not telling me something, Ava. It's not like you to act this way."

My eyes rounded. "Act what way?"

His fingers thrummed the steering wheel before he started the engine and steered the car between traffic, weaving in and out of lanes as though in a hurry to get back to the hotel.

I didn't want to fight. I reached over and stroked his thigh, feeling strong muscles beneath his trousers. He adjusted the air conditioner, ignoring my touch. I decided to try a different angle. "How did your mother meet your father? I know she's Australian. Did they meet here?"

He nodded. "Yeah, they did. And yet my Australian grandmother met my grandfather in India. She was touring India with her girlfriend and toward the end of her tour, she went to a cricket game. Australia versus India." He grinned. "A few days later, both my grandmother and her friend attended a wedding celebration. She struggled to keep up with the dance steps in her sari. My grandfather introduced himself and offered to guide her through the steps. She recognised him and, of course, fell for his charm."

I knew all too well about falling for the Kumble charm.

"Before my grandfather died, he told me that my grandmother was the most beautiful woman he'd laid eyes on. He said it was love at first sight." He smirked. "Like you and me." He pulled up at a red light and placed his hand on my bare thigh. His gaze went to where his fingers lingered at the hem of my dress and then he looked up and met my gaze, his beautiful brown eyes twinkling in the light of oncoming traffic. "Though I can't imagine anyone feeling what I am right now."

"What's that?" I croaked.

"That I can't get enough of you." He almost growled. "You have a hold on me. One I can't control. Every second of the day, I think about you."

My heart sped up when his fingers slipped under the material.

"I know you feel it too," he whispered. His gaze bore into me. "Don't deny it. What we have is strong. It's as though we're meant for each other," he said in a quiet voice.

"I feel it." My hand wrapped around his. "And I never want you to stop wanting me."

"I don't think I could, even if I tried." For a few seconds, we stared at each other, channelling our emotions. Then a horn sounded behind, startling us both. I giggled, and Jardine removed his hand before planting his foot on the accelerator with more force than necessary.

A sense of urgency to get to the hotel took over. Once inside the elevator, Jardine pushed me against the wall, his hands roaming over my butt as his lips devoured me. He moaned against my lips and then the bell chimed, alerting us that we'd reached our floor. My whole body tingled in anticipation as we walked toward our room. The door closed behind me and Jardine swept me effortlessly into his arms and carried me to the bed.

Before he lowered me onto the covers, I reached up and placed a hand on his cheek. Our eyes met. "I love you," I breathed. He stood frozen to the spot. He closed his eyes and pushed his face into my hand.

"Thank you." He opened his eyes and lowered me onto the bed. "I'm going to show you how much I'm in love with you, Ava Walters."

I smiled at his use of my full name. The wine made me playful and brave. I scrambled to the centre of the bed, pulled off my panties, and opened my legs to him.

Jardine's eyes widened. His fingers made quick work of his zipper, followed by the buttons on his shirt. As soon as he rid himself of his clothes, Jardine sprang onto the bed and pressed his long lean body into me, kissed me in a way I lost all coherent thought.

CHAPTER 5

Daylight streamed into the room. Jardine had left the curtains open—again. There was something romantic about looking out a window to city lights while making love. But come morning, the romance of an open window evaporated when sunlight burned my eyes.

My eyelashes fluttered open. This weekend had seemed like a dream. Jardine and I were closer and more into each other than ever, if that were even possible. I rolled over to face him and withheld a groan. The pain of overused and overstretched muscles reminded me it was real.

"Good morning," I whispered and kissed his cheek. Jardine lifted an arm and I snuggled into his side. "How long have you been awake?"

"Awhile."

"I've had fun." My hand rested on his sculptured abs. "Can't we stay longer?"

Jardine turned his head and kissed my forehead. "I wish. But honestly, you've wrecked me. I've got nothing left in the tank."

I giggled. "Finally. It's nice lying here next to you. Just the two of us."

"I know," he said. "I've been thinking about that. Us having our own place."

I looked up at him. "I don't think our parents would agree to it." I swallowed, thinking of my own parents' reactions. Since I didn't have a job and I wanted to study, I doubted they'd allow me to shack up with Jardine. And his parents… hell would freeze over before his father would allow it. "I thought we were trying to get into the same university?"

He nodded and looked directly ahead at the wall. "I'm just thinking."

"Well, it's a nice thought. One day we'll have our dream."

More time passed and neither one of us moved, holding the other as though in our own universe and time had momentarily stilled. I was afraid to let go, knowing that when I did, our perfect world would shift back to reality.

Cleo was right. By letting myself go, I'd opened up to Jardine. We were definitely closer on a physical level. He now understood me, understood my needs, emotionally and sexually, and I felt like a different person.

I ran a finger along his abs, tracing the outline of each muscle. "You know, last night you never told me how your parents met. Only your grandparents."

He turned his head and gawked at me. "Really? You want to talk about that now when we only have a short time left to enjoy each other?"

"We have enjoyed each other. I've learned some things." I grinned and walked my fingers down his stomach. "I want to know about your family." I kissed his shoulder.

"What about your family?" he murmured.

I snorted. "You know everything about my family since you're always at my house. And you've heard my dad tell the story how he first saw my mother in church."

Jardine chuckled under his breath and my head shook on his chest. "We would never have met there. I'm thankful I moved to Adelaide and to your school."

"Me too," I whispered. I thrummed my fingers on his chest. "Your parents?"

His chest rose and fell. "My father worked at a hospital in Sydney, where my mum worked as a nurse. After a few weeks, he finally worked up the courage to ask her out." He laughed, more so to himself. "Their first date was at a restaurant at Bondi. Strange that a surfy chick intimidated him."

I gaped at him. "Your mum surfed?"

Jardine's mother was blonde, blue-eyed, tanned, and even now, stunningly beautiful. I found her easy to talk to, but she also carried a sense of refinement about her. Especially the way she held her head high and her shoulders back. Unlike me, she never slouched.

Well, now she was cool as well as classy.

"Yeah. Even though my dad acts like a tool at times with his head stuck up his rear, he fell hard for my mum." He rubbed the side of his face. "My grandfather wanted him to marry a nice Indian girl, but my grandmother told dad to follow his heart and for my grandfather to keep his nose out of it." He grinned and turned on his side to face me. "Looks like the Kumbles have a weakness for beautiful Australian women."

I pulled a face at him. "That's the worst pickup line ever."

He rubbed his nose with mine. "You like it."

I moaned, defeated when Jardine made me feel special. I kissed his cheek. "I knew this weekend would bring us closer, even though we've always been close." I looked up into his eyes. "But now I feel so connected to you. It's like I've shared my..." I said the only word that came to mind, "soul."

Jardine pulled me into his arms, our naked bodies curled around the other like vines. "And you have mine. I promise, I'll always be there. You are my everything, Ava."

Reality hit —hard. Jardine stayed away the next few days and I caught up on my neglected chores at home. He sent countless texts telling me he loved me. Every night, I received the same text.

> *Wish you were here lying next to me. I miss you. Sweet dreams xx*
> *I love you <3*

On the third day, I called him.

"I miss you so much it hurts," I breathed into the phone.

"I miss you too. My body misses you. Nights will never be the same."

"Where are you?"

"With my mum. We're filling out forms. I had a medical today. Standard procedure. Cricket stuff."

"Oh. What's happening this weekend?"

"The Red Birds play interstate this weekend, so I'll be away regardless of which team I'm selected for. I want to see you before I go. Can we go to the movies?"

"Of course." I didn't care where we went; I only wanted to see him.

"I know it's not much, but I'm tired. Training has been intense this week. And after the weekend..." his voice trailed away. "I want to see you."

"I'll do anything you want."

"Okay. I'll call after training. I love you, Ava."

"And I love you."

I flopped back on my bed. I needed to fill my time so I wasn't constantly thinking of Jardine. I tapped on Cleo's number and sent a message.

Want to go for a walk along the beach?

A few hours later, Cleo and I strolled into a café after our walk. We ordered and sat at a table near the street.

"Okay, tell me everything. How was your weekend? How's Jardine?" She wiggled her eyebrows suggestively.

I rolled my eyes. "Oh, you know. Wonderful. Perfect. Great sex." I giggled.

Cleo leaned back in her seat. Her eyes widened. "Go on."

I gave her a wry smile. "You know, I surprised myself. I never thought I could..." I trailed off.

"I get it," Cleo interrupted. "You two couldn't keep your hands off each other. So what's lover boy up to this week?"

I filled Cleo in on the latest cricket update and told her about Jardine's father.

"I'm scared. What if he's selected to play for Australia? He'll be away most of the year. I hear things about sports players on trips."

Cleo raised her hand. "Are you suggesting Jardine will cheat on you?"

I shrugged. "If he's away for months at a time and if hot girls are always in his face... I don't know."

"Well, I can tell you now Jardine only has eyes for you." She tilted her head. "Surely he told you himself."

I nodded. "But we're talking *months* here. He'll be with the elite cricketers of the world and girls will flock to them. I'm just saying it'll be hard only seeing him a couple of months of the year. Honestly, I'd be selfish to want him to myself. I can't expect him not to have fun with his team. I'd be holding him back."

It hurt saying it out loud. I tried to be the bigger person, but my heart raced with the number of emotions flowing through me. Especially jealousy and anger as I imagined other girls hanging around him. I clenched my fists. Then I reminded myself how old we were. I loved him with all my heart and wanted him to have his dream, but... could I do it?

"You're being ridiculous." Cleo folded her arms over her chest. "Seriously. There are guys on the team who are married. You don't think they're cheating, do you?"

"I don't expect him to hang out with the older guys just to remain faithful to me. It's not fair on him."

Cleo shook her head. "Would you remain faithful if it were you?"

"Of course."

She rolled her eyes. "Well, like you said, nothing is set yet. No need to worry about something that mightn't happen."

I nodded, ignoring the gnawing feeling in my gut.

"This weekend, the whole gang is going out. Come. You haven't been out with us in ages."

I stalled a moment. "Who?"

"Chelsea, Abigail, Oliver, Callum and Ewan. All of us."

"Except Jardine." I sighed. "Well, since he's away... okay."

Cleo clapped her hands. "Yay. I promise, we'll have so much fun you won't even think about Jardine."

Sitting in the back row of a dark cinema, I held onto Jardine's hand in my lap, his head resting on my shoulder. He hadn't moved in a while so I assumed he'd fallen asleep. The credits rolled across the screen and yet he remained still. I kissed the top of his head.

Slowly, he lifted his head and blinked at the screen. Dimmed lights brightened and he turned to me with apologetic eyes.

"Worse date ever, huh?"

"Never. I'm happy we could be together." I kissed his cheek. "I'd rather be with you asleep than not at all. Does that make me selfish, dragging you out when you should be in bed?"

His hand cupped my cheek. "I'd rather have you in my bed," he murmured against my lips.

"When will we get another chance? I mean, with your cricket and my parents checking on us, it'll be a while." I wrapped my arms around his neck and kissed him, showing him how much he meant to me and not caring who saw.

We strolled back to his car, savouring every minute together. Jardine's flight to Melbourne was tomorrow. I wouldn't see him again until Monday. Already I struggled with not seeing him and deep down prayed that he'd never make the Australian team, knowing I couldn't cope with the separation.

Selfish?

Yes.

Inside his car, I rubbed his thigh, needing to touch him. We pulled up outside of my house and Jardine killed the engine.

"You want to come in?"

Jardine shook his head. "I'm wiped, and I have to get up for an early morning flight." He leaned across and nibbled on my neck. "Promise I'll make it up to you when I get back."

"I'll hold you to it," I whispered. I arched my neck, encouraging him to take more of me. His lips trailed a line to my lips and then he kissed me tenderly. I pulled away and rubbed my nose with his. "Good luck, sweetheart. Hope you win."

Jardine grabbed both of my hands and kissed the back of each. "I'll miss you. See you when I get back."

I nodded. "Call me when you can." Then, I turned and stepped out of the car. Jardine started the engine and waited until I reached the front door before leaving. As soon I unlocked the door, I pivoted and waved to him. My heart ached and my whole body turned limp watching Jardine drive away. It was only for the weekend, but it signified more. Like the beginning to our end. I stood there until his car turned out of my street, swiping at the tears pooling in my eyes.

How the hell would I cope with him gone months at a time?

CHAPTER 6

Cleo's favourite DJ remix blared through the speakers in her bedroom. Strangely, my mood was light and happy, even though Jardine wouldn't be there. We were meeting up with the rest of the gang later at a club. As I applied mascara to my lashes and hummed along to a song, she bounced over to me and placed another bottle of vodka and raspberry in my hand. "Let's get dressed and hang outside with Yasmine and her friends."

"Sure." I liked Cleo's sister and her friends and enjoyed listening to their stories. Only four years older, yet they seemed smarter and much more worldly.

"Hey." Yasmine smiled. "You must be relieved exams are over and there's no studying 'til next year?"

"Oh God, yes. Though the celebrations will continue every weekend for a while, I imagine." I looked at Cleo and grinned while raising my hand, holding the fourth bottle of vodka and soda I'd consumed.

We joined the girls and I cringed at the board game on the table. I hated drinking games. Eden, Yasmine's bestie, must have noticed as she commented, "We've finished playing." She smiled at me. "But who is up for a game of 'Who Would You?'"

"Wait a few minutes until Chelsea and Abi get here?" Cleo said quickly. Thankfully, it bought me some time. Cleo finished her drink and extended her hand to me, suggesting I down my drink. If I had to play these games, I needed some liquid courage. My arms hung like a lead weight, but I still wasn't drunk enough to play this game.

Cleo headed to the ice bucket to get more cans and I tuned in to Eden and Yasmine, who were chatting about a holiday. Yasmine was suggesting that they leave in February. My ears pricked. "Where are you girls heading?"

"South America," Eden replied. "Number one for me is to visit the Amazon rainforest, but Yasmine wants to go to Carnival in Rio de Janeiro." She rolled her eyes. "It'll cost a damn fortune!"

"We've been saving for years, Eden. It's a once-in-a-lifetime experience. Imagine all the hot Brazilian men." Yasmine's face changed as though she'd just had an orgasm. I looked at Eden.

"The best part is we get to go to a ceremony for Yemaya. It would complete the trip for me." She looked sideways at Yasmine. "We just have to convince Rella it's not all about partying and hot men!"

Cleo sat back down and placed another drink in front of me. "Not the holiday again. Just do it already."

"We are," Yasmine snapped and took a sip from her wine glass. "We have an appointment Monday at a travel company to finalise our itinerary."

"So you're heading overseas next year? How exciting. How long are you going?" I asked, completely in awe.

Yasmine glared at Cleo. "I haven't told Mum, but we're staying a few months."

"You mentioned four weeks."

Yasmine nodded. "I know. I've decided to resign from work, then I'll apply for another job when I get back."

Abigail and Chelsea came through the side gate, interrupting the conversation. "Hi," they sung in tune.

Eden clapped. "Grab a drink, girls. We've been waiting for you to show up so we can start a game of 'Who Would You?'"

"Awesome," I murmured.

Yasmine swirled the wine in her glass and peered into it as though it held her answers. "I'll start. Who would I marry? Um, Harri. Who Would I kill? Err, Joffrey on *Game of Thrones*."

"That's cheating," Eden interrupted. "It has to be someone you know."

Yasmine rolled her eyes. "Fine, my boss because he gives me the worst shifts."

Eden groaned before tapping the table with her fingertips in a rhythmic drumroll for the next answer.

Yasmine laughed. "And who would I fuck? Darcy Rayne."

"That's too obvious," Eden said quickly. "We all notice the way you look at him in the club."

"Yeah well he's a footballer with a huge circle of girls shrouding him. Hard to break that ring of lust." Yasmine drained the remainder of her wine. "And sports players never play fair when it comes to your heart. Anyways, you're next, Eden." She refilled their glasses.

Eden named two guys, one who she'd marry and one who she'd kill. I didn't recognise either. The point of the game seemed to be revealing the guy you wanted to fuck. Therein lay the truth—marrying and killing someone deemed irrelevant and unimportant.

"Who would I screw?"

"Fuck," Yasmine corrected.

"I don't like that word." Eden raised a brow and Yasmine coughed. "There's actually no one who turns me on at the moment."

"Come on," Yasmine whined. "What about your ex? He's doable. And you did it with him a lot!"

"Ethan? No. It needs to be someone I pine for, right? I'll pass."

"Whatever. Skol," Yasmine demanded.

Eden shrugged and downed her drink. She turned to me. "Ava?"

My vodka bottle suddenly became the most fascinating thing around me. I twirled it in my fingers. "My answers aren't interesting. Who would I marry? Jardine, of course. Who would I kill? The person who thought exams was a good way to calculate intelligence."

"Boring," Cleo chimed.

I shrugged. "It passes. And who would I fuck?" I grinned at Eden. "Easy. Jardine."

"No," everyone screamed at once.

"Doesn't count." Chelsea grinned. "You can't name the same person twice."

"Wait, what?" I gasped. "There is no one else."

"Come on," Eden said. "What about that guy who's been in love with you since preschool?"

"Huh?" I gaped at her. "Who?"

"Oliver," Cleo answered for me. "You know he's always had a thing for you."

"Um, no. We're good friends. Like brother and sister." I looked around the group, seeking support.

Abigail raised her eyebrows. "To you, maybe."

I stared at Cleo. She nodded her head in confirmation. My heart raced and memories of our times together flashed through my mind as I searched for clues. Oliver had always been there for me...as a friend. Or so I'd thought.

I wiped my hands on my dress. "I'll skol."

My head swirled after finishing my drink. My friends' responses faded away as I thought of Oliver holding my hand and hugging me whenever I felt down. Part of me felt betrayed, the other part confused. How the hell was I supposed to act when we were meeting up with him in a matter of minutes? I decided to drink water for the remainder of the night.

Cleo grabbed my hand and pulled me away from the dance floor. "Let's get a drink. I'm wrecked."

"I'm only drinking water," I said quickly. I'd managed to avoid any long conversations with Oliver, other than a few random comments. I wanted to keep my wits in case he tried anything. I doubt he would but my drunken thoughts were erratic. A wave of nausea hit me for thinking unkindly of Oliver. In all the time I'd known him, he had never tried to hit on me. He respected our friendship and I valued him as a friend. My gaze caught his as I strolled from the dance floor toward the bar, where the remainder of my friends had gathered. He walked up to me and put an arm around my shoulder. I closed my eyes and tried not to look into it further.

"What do you girls want to drink?" he asked.

"I'll have a vodka," Cleo said before lifting his other arm and placing it over her shoulder.

"Water for me." I gazed up at him and smiled in an effort to appear nonchalant.

"No worries. Be back soon."

"He's a darling," Cleo commented.

"He is," I added. Was I overreacting?

Oliver arrived back within minutes, carrying a vodka shot and a bottle of Evian. He handed the shot to Cleo. "For you, sweetness."

Callum joined us and Cleo winked at me. "Bottoms up." After downing her drink, she stood on her toes and planted a kiss on Oliver's cheek before turning to Callum. "Want to dance?"

What the –? She said she was wrecked!

I glanced at Oliver and smiled awkwardly when Cleo and Callum headed to the dance floor.

"Okay," he said. "Something's up with you. I know Jardine's away, but you've been acting weird all night."

My chin dipped. I hated the awkwardness between us. I glanced over my shoulder at our friends. Ewan stumbled toward Chelsea and leaned in close. She pushed him away. Thankfully, I'd managed to avoid him tonight. Everyone was out of earshot. "Can we go outside and talk?" I asked, not wanting to shout over the music.

His eyes studied me a moment. "Sure."

Outside, I breathed in the cool air, a welcome relief from the stuffy overheated nightclub.

We walked around the corner to an alley. I leaned back against the brick wall, my hands clasped behind my back. Staring at the stained cement, I inhaled a deep breath. "I heard you've had a major crush on me since forever. Is it true?"

Oliver coughed. "Shit, Ava, could you be any more blunt?"

I shrugged. "Is it?"

Oliver stepped away from me, putting some distance between us. My insides clenched as panic grew. "Oliver, I'm not mad."

He looked at me and I couldn't tell if he was angry. "You've been acting weird all night. Maybe you're not mad, but something's up. When did you find out? Tonight?"

I nodded. "It confused me. We've been friends for a long time. I trust you."

Oliver scratched the back of his neck. "We are. But I've always been attracted to you. I thought you knew that? I'd never make you choose between Jardine and me, because I know you'd choose him." I nodded. "But I'm here for you...like a brother. You're also my friend. I'd never hurt you, Ava." He closed the gap and pulled me into his chest. At first it felt wrong, but then familiarity warmed me and I snuggled into him.

"I'm sorry. I never wanted anything to come between us." I felt him kiss my hair. "Tell me. Why do you and Jardine not like each other?"

"He hasn't told you?"

"No," I said into his blue shirt.

"He knows, and he should be the one to say."

I nodded, yet didn't let go of him. "No matter what happens, I want us to remain friends." I leaned back. "We'll always be friends, right?"

"Friends with benefits?" he joked.

"No." I shook my head and giggled.

He released me. "I need to piss. Wait here."

Oliver walked around the far corner to somewhere private. I turned the opposite way to find Ewan walking toward me.

"What are you doing out here?" he slurred.

I stepped away from him and backed up against the wall. "I'm chatting with Oliver. He's gone to pee." I nodded in the direction where Oliver had disappeared.

He took a step closer. "Why are you alone with Oliver? Does Jardine know?" he asked, taking another step toward me.

"Oliver and I are just talking. That's all." My heart sped up when he closed the gap between us. "I think I'll wait for Oliver inside." I stepped to the side, away from him.

Ewan slammed both hands on either side of my head.

"Really? I think you came out here to get some action with Oliver while your boy's away." I shook my head and whimpered at how close his face was to mine. His foul breath wafted over me. The smell of alcohol and old pizza made me want to puke. "You wear this dress for me?"

"No," I said quickly and placed my hands firmly on his chest, ready to push him. "Go away, Ewan."

He glanced down at my hands and snickered, as though I was no match compared to his strength. He pushed the weight of his body against mine as he kissed me. I tried to struggle, moving my head side-to-side, but the brick wall scratched the back of my head. "No," I tried to say against his disgusting mouth. Panic clawed its way up my throat when his hand went between my legs and under my dress. I yelled at him and shoved hard.

For a moment, I thought I'd developed a superpower as he flew into the air and landed in a heap on the ground. Then I saw Oliver standing over him. I let out a sob and straightened my dress.

"What the fuck, man? What's the matter with you?" Oliver turned back to me, gaping. I burst into tears, coughing and wiping my mouth with my hand. Oliver strode to my side and wrapped his arms around me. "What happened?"

I shook my head. "I don't know. He walked up to me when you left, and forced himself on me."

Ewan groaned and Oliver released me. He swung around. "What the fuck were you thinking?"

Ewan stood, stumbled back, and wiped his mouth. "She asked me to kiss her, mate. Serious."

"You're lying. And you weren't just kissing her," Oliver growled. "It's taking all my energy not to smash your face right now."

I grabbed Oliver's arm. "Don't. He's not worth it."

"She's a slut. We all know it."

Oliver flew at him and I screamed. "Don't, Oliver. He's drunk and he won't remember a thing tomorrow."

Oliver had Ewan by the collar of his shirt, his other arm poised like he had an arrow ready to fire. He turned his head to me. "Do you want to press charges?"

I shook my head, my thoughts churning. Ewan was Jardine's friend. Their parents were on the school board together. It was his word against mine. We were both drunk. Did I want to go to the police? My parents would never let me out again. "Tell him never to come near me again."

"You heard her," Oliver warned. "You ever go near Ava, I will not only beat you, I will make sure she presses charges. Understand?" Oliver pushed Ewan away and I watched as Ewan stumbled down the alley, mumbling to himself.

Oliver came to me and hugged me tightly. "Did he hurt you? I couldn't see, but did he...?"

"No," I croaked. Tears streamed down my cheeks. Oliver didn't see anything but a drunken kiss. "He scared me. He's always scared me."

"You're safe now. Ssh...I'll get you home."

Oliver held onto me, taking some of my weight as we headed to the taxi stop. He kissed the top of my head. "Are you going to tell anyone about this? Your parents?"

I shook my head. "If you hadn't come along, it could've been worse. If I tell my parents, they'll freak and ban me from going out. I'll tell Cleo. No one else."

"No one else?" his voice croaked.

"No. Just the three of us. If Jardine finds out..." I shook my head. "I doubt Ewan will even remember. But I never want to see him again to find out. I'll make sure Cleo never tells as well. I don't want this getting around. It'll look bad for me."

"It'll look bad for Ewan, not you." He grabbed my hand and squeezed it. "It wasn't your fault. He was drunk, but he's always been an ass."

"I hate him." I swiped away tears and buried my face into Oliver's chest.

CHAPTER 7

We won, which is the only upside to being away from you. I've missed you, babe. I'm sitting here at the airport listening to some of the guys talking about hitting the Shores nightclub tonight. So glad there's no school tomorrow! How was your weekend? Can't wait to see you. Love you xxx

My hand shook as I read Jardine's message. "I miss you too," I said quietly to myself. I rolled over in bed and squeezed my eyes shut. If only Jardine had been here last night...

Was Ewan going to rape me?

I shook my head, blocking the image of his hands all over me, his stinking breath in my face.

Why? Ewan didn't even like me.

I lifted my fingers and pressed the corner of my eyes to stop the tears.

Did Ewan remember?

The thought lingered.

"This is bullshit," I murmured. I threw back the covers and jumped out of bed. I was better than this. I wasn't going to let him bring me down. Not when my boyfriend would be home soon. And if Ewan were to come near me again, I'd be ready. Besides, Oliver would kill him.

I flopped back onto the bed.

Oliver.

I definitely felt something for him. Not what I felt for Jardine, but I couldn't deny I had feelings. Somehow I knew Oliver would *always* be there for me.

I grabbed my phone and sent a text to Jardine.

I miss you too. Glad you won! Weekend was okay. Looking forward to seeing you soon xxx

Then I sent Cleo a message.

How was your night with Callum? Sorry I left without saying goodbye. Oliver and I caught a cab together so all good. Do you want to meet for breakfast?

Cleo replied immediately, asking to meet at the Bay in an hour. Then I tapped on Oliver's name. The last time I sent him a message was in July, asking him about an English assignment. My shoulders sagged as I realised I only texted him when I wanted something.

Hey, thanks for last night. Don't know what I'd do without you. You're the best-est friend. I love you xx

As I grabbed some clean clothes to head to the shower, my phone vibrated on the bedside table with an incoming call. Oliver.

"Hey. Thank you," I said in a calm voice, hoping my tone and those two words conveyed everything my heart felt for him.

"How are you today?" I heard the concern in his voice.

"I'm okay. Better. Kinda figured Ewan was drunk and not in control. I understand it wasn't my fault. I was in the wrong place at the wrong time."

The line went silent. "Oliver?"

"Yeah, sorry. It doesn't excuse his actions. I want to go 'round and see him, but not without your permission."

I sucked in a deep breath. "No. I want to forget it. The more I think about it, the more it sickens me. *If* he remembers, then I'll expect an apology and a promise he'll never touch me again."

"You deserve that, even if he doesn't remember." His voice sounded louder...angrier.

"Oliver," I whispered. "Let's just wait and see."

"I won't forgive the bastard for this. One day I'll make him pay for what he did."

"Not now. Please." I held the side of my head, hoping to relieve the pressure of a thumping headache.

"Fine. Tell me if you need anything."

"Well, I'm catching up with Cleo for coffee if you want to join us."

He coughed. "And hear all the gory details about Cleo with Callum? I'll pass."

I giggled into the phone.

"That's a sound I enjoy hearing. You have a good time. Oh, and Ava...I love you too."

Then I ended the call.

Shit. I loved Oliver but not how I loved Jardine. One thing's for sure, no way would I push Oliver away because of his feelings for me—I cared too deeply to hurt him. And after last night, I valued his friendship even more.

Cleo pushed ringlets behind her ear. "Did I tell you his father owns a holiday house in Byron Bay and he has invited me to visit over the summer?"

"Yeah. Twice." I smirked at my friend. Lust at our age took over our every thought...and common sense. I sipped my latte, the second in a couple of hours.

"Sorry." Cleo gave me a goofy smile. "You haven't said a word about last night. So why did you guys leave so early?"

My stomach clenched. "I felt sick and Oliver mentioned he was tired, so we caught a cab together to save money."

"Nothing you want to tell me about Oliver?"

My throat tightened. Not about Oliver. I'd made progress this morning and didn't want to relive the nightmare with Ewan. Cleo would hate me not telling her, but I couldn't force myself to talk about it. "No." I frowned at her. "Oliver is like a brother to me. You know that."

"I do. But after you found out about his feelings, I thought..."

"Don't," I snapped. "I could never cheat on Jardine. I love him too much." I closed my eyes momentarily. "Seriously. I thought you understood us?"

"I do," Cleo added quickly. "It was stupid of me to say. I know how good you and Jardine are together. Speaking of, when does he get back?"

I checked the time on my phone. "I expect he's home now. I should go." I picked up my bag from the ground and shoved my phone inside the pocket. "I'll call you soon." I kissed Cleo on the cheek. "What are your plans for the week?"

She grinned. "Mum has given me a list of chores, but I'm sending out some résumés, looking for part-time work until uni starts."

"I'll come over and we can send letters out together. Not sure what I'm going to do until then. I'm not staying home. Mum drives me nuts. And I need a backup plan. If I don't get into med school..."

"Stop. No negative thoughts. You sent the letter to Yemaya. It's out of your hands. What will be, will be."

I turned my wrist and stared at the words inked across my wrist. "Yes. Que Sera." I gave her a knowing smile. "Call you tomorrow."

"Good, you're home," Dad said as soon as I walked in the front door. "Go and get changed for mass."

"What? Jardine is coming over—"

"I expect you to attend church tonight with your family, Ava. You skipped last week and other Sundays because of exams." His lips pressed tight. "The excuse of your boyfriend coming over is not convincing. Is something going on with you I'm not aware of?"

"No, Dad. You know Jardine has been away, and now he'll be travelling, we don't get to see each other much. Please."

"And this is God's fault?" Dad glanced at his watch. "Why don't you ask Jardine to come with us?"

I coughed. "Jardine is not Catholic, Dad. He's kinda Hindu."

"Kinda? Well, let me tell you, young lady, I don't ever want to hear you're *kinda* Catholic. We agreed to allow you to go to a non-Catholic school, but we did not agree to you abandoning your beliefs."

I swallowed and looked away from my father's intense gaze. If ever I was to feel guilty about my relationship with Jardine—especially our weekend together—now was the time.

No. I was wrong.

Guilt weighed heavily on my shoulders as I sat alongside my parents in church, staring at the paintings of Christ on the cross and a statue with his arms held out to his side, embracing and forgiving.

I had called Jardine and explained to him how important it was to my dad that I attend church. What surprised me was his eagerness to attend mass with me, except he'd be late.

My phone vibrated in my bag next to me, out of sight of my father. I checked the message.

I'm here xx

I slowly turned my head and checked the main door. Jardine made his way along the side of the church toward my row. I dropped my phone back into my bag and shifted to create a space for him. My father frowned at me when Jardine squeezed past him to sit with me.

"Sorry," I whispered, knowing how my father hated tardiness, especially in church.

"One hour of your time once a week is not too much to ask," he would say when I was young.

Jardine kissed my cheek and grabbed my hand. "I've missed you."

I smiled and squeezed his hand, unable to prevent the heat creeping up my neck to my cheeks. All I could think about was what I did with this man in bed not so long ago. I could sense Dad staring at me, but I refused to look at him, convinced I-had-crazy-sex-with-my-boyfriend was engraved across my scarlet cheeks.

Throughout the service, I'd glance at Jardine, checking to see if he was keeping up—or more so, that he didn't look uncomfortable. Whenever a prayer required a response, Jardine answered dutifully. My heart swelled, knowing he would do this for me.

When mass ended, Mum asked Jardine back for supper, at which time Dad quizzed Jardine about his game, the players, and the general goings-on at elite-level cricket. Jardine answered without showing any signs of being uncomfortable by his intrusive questions and avoided divulging 'inside' information about sports stars.

"You know, I'm craving chocolate," I said quickly before Dad could ask Jardine another question. "Do you want to come to the shop with me?" I smiled at Jardine.

His shoulders relaxed. "Sure."

Inside his car he kissed me, long and hard. "Wow. I thought I'd never get you alone," he said against my lips.

I kissed his cheek. "I know. Thank you for coming to church, for answering all those questions, for… everything."

"Everything?" He raised a brow.

"For loving me."

Jardine cupped my face with his hands "You have no idea how much." Then he leaned in and kissed me, this time slow and gentle.

Jardine pulled away and started the engine. "Where are we going?"

"To buy chocolate," I replied, grinning.

"Serious?"

"Yeah. Oddly enough, I'm craving it."

Jardine laughed and steered the car onto the road. "I was thinking of a deserted car park."

I reached across and rubbed his thigh. "You could probably convince me to do anything after chocolate." I gave him my best come-to-bed-with-me smile.

"Anything? Then I vote chocolate as your staple diet."

I laughed and gazed out the window to the quiet suburban street, daydreaming about what we could do in his car.

Jardine parked the car in front of the shop and handed me a twenty-dollar note. "Get enough for the week." He wiggled his brows.

"A week? I'll need more than a twenty," I joked.

After buying two blocks of chocolate, I headed toward the car and caught a glimpse of Jardine, sitting behind the wheel, playing on his phone.

I jumped in the passenger seat and froze when I saw it was my phone. Jardine stared at me with a stony expression, and for a moment neither of us spoke. I had nothing to hide, yet his expression told me otherwise.

Jardine turned the screen to me. "When did you start telling Oliver you love him? And what did he do for you last night?"

I gaped at him. "What?"

"I think you heard me." He moved the phone closer as though it would clarify any confusion.

I grabbed the phone from his grasp and read the message I'd sent to Oliver, thankful he'd called me instead of replying to my text when he told me he loved me too. Not that it was the kind of love Jardine assumed.

I lifted my gaze to Jardine and saw his brow pinched in a V. "It's not what you think." I maintained an even tone despite the memories of last night causing my throat to turn dry.

"Really? You sent a text to Oliver saying you love him and yet he didn't reciprocate. I know he wants you, so what the fuck is going on?"

I froze at his tone. The memory of Ewan pushing himself onto me made me nauseous. Jardine stared angrily at me, waiting, and in my mind I saw Ewan groping me.

Not my fault.

"I should be angry that you violated my privacy and read my messages."

"Especially when you're hiding something. Have I found out your dirty little secret?" he asked sarcastically.

I cringed at his tone. "No, you haven't found out my dirty little secret. Only Oliver knows that. Like I said, it's not what you think." I turned away to face the window as tears welled in my eyes.

"Take me home." So many emotions ran through me. Hurt. Anger. Frustration. Panic. How could Jardine think I was capable of loving anyone but him?

Jardine slammed the gear stick into drive and pulled out onto the road faster than necessary.

I inhaled a deep breath. "I didn't know how to tell you without making you angry. And I didn't want to distract you from cricket." I kept my head turned away from him. I raised my hand closest to the door and trapped a tear with one finger as it trickled down my cheek.

"What the hell are you talking about?"

I twisted in my seat to face him and wished I hadn't when I caught sight of his expression. His eyes were stormy and his face was red, not with embarrassment but with anger I'd never seen before. The Jardine I knew was gentle, loving and full of encouragement, not cold and full of wrath.

We were having our first real fight and all because of a misunderstanding. I reached out and touched his leg. He gave me a sideways glance, his expression serious, before looking back to the road.

"Last night someone tried to..." How did I explain this to him when he was this furious, especially while driving? "Well, Oliver stopped something bad from happening to me. I was so thankful he was there because..." I couldn't say the words. "And I told him I loved him, meaning as a friend." I looked down at my hands quivering in my lap.

The car's rear spun out as Jardine navigated a sharp corner without slowing. He swerved to the side of the road and killed the engine. He turned in his seat, one hand clutching the steering wheel like a life support, the other still resting on the gear stick in park. "What did someone try to do?"

"Touch me." The words come out in a whisper.

His fingers tightened around the steering wheel. "Who?"

"Some drunk idiot. I was so scared." Tears streamed down my cheeks.

Jardine pulled me into his chest, his strong arms wrapping around me, holding me tight. "Why didn't you tell me?" he rasped.

"I wanted to. Guess I was waiting for the right time, or maybe I just wanted to forget."

"Tell me what happened?"

I leaned back and he released me. He picked up my hand and massaged it, soothing me. I swallowed the lump growing in my throat. Jardine knew I went out with the gang as I had sent him a text from Cleo's. "It was getting late and I went outside to talk to Oliver."

"About what?"

"Him liking me." My bottom lip quivered.

Jardine closed his eyes and then opened them again. "Go on."

"I told him I was in love with you. He understood and respects our relationship. He said he'd never get between us. He's not the type of guy to break people up."

"Love makes people do crazy shit."

"No. He'd never come between us; never make me choose. He knows I'd choose you."

Jardine didn't say anything. He picked up my hand and kissed it. "What did he do?"

"Oliver?"

"No. The drunk."

I bit my lip. "Oliver walked around the corner to pee, and," I stalled, "*he* saw I was alone and came up to me. I went to walk away, then he had me trapped against the wall. Next thing I knew, he was kissing me. I tried yanking my head back and hit the wall. His hot, stinking breath was all over me. It was gross." I closed my eyes, remembering Ewan's foul breath and his hands...

I trembled. Jardine pulled me into his arms again. "I'm so sorry, babe." His large hand cradled the back of my head. "So sorry I wasn't there." His fingers massaged my head. "Did he do anything else?" he asked in a throaty voice.

I nodded against his shoulder. "He tried to touch me."

"What do you mean *tried*?"

"He forced himself on me. Then his hand went under my dress to my panties." Jardine stiffened against me.

"Did. He?" he managed.

I shook my head. "I pushed him away, and at the same time Oliver appeared and threw him off me. They got in a fight, but I stopped Oliver from hitting him. Then I asked him to take me home. He wanted to call the police, but I refused."

He grabbed both of my shoulders and looked into my eyes. "Why?"

I knew if Jardine ever found out I'd lied about it being Ewan, he'd be furious. And yet I couldn't find the guts to tell him, knowing how he'd react. Everything would come to a head and I wasn't ready to face Ewan. I just wanted it all to go away. "At the end of the day, it was a drunk guy who wouldn't even remember what he did. I was at the wrong place at the wrong time," I said, repeating the words I'd told Oliver. "I'm so sorry." I fell forward into his chest.

Jardine's arms squeezed me in a bear hug. "Ssh. It's okay now, babe. I'm home. I'm here."

"I missed you," I whimpered.

"I owe you and Oliver an apology."

"You didn't know. I'm sorry for keeping it from you."

"Ssh." He kissed the top of my head.

We remained huddled together for another ten minutes before he drove me home. Outside my house, Jardine leaned over and kissed me tenderly on the lips.

"I'll call you first thing tomorrow. Do you have anything planned?"

I shook my head. "Do you have training?"

"Not 'til the evening." He kissed my cheek, his lips grazing my ear. "I love you."

"I love you too." I kissed his lips before stepping out of the car. Like every other time, Jardine waited until I was inside before driving away.

CHAPTER 8

Thankfully, my parents were in bed when I walked into the house.

Lying in the dark, I scrolled through photos on my iPhone of Jardine and me…at school, at the beach, in my bedroom, goofing around. Life seemed so much simpler only a few months ago.

My finger stilled over an image of Jardine hugging me, his arm outstretched as he took a selfie. I smiled at his fun-loving expression. My phone vibrated with an incoming call, startling me.

I swiped the screen to accept Oliver's call.

"Hey, what's up?"

"Sorry I'm calling late. Um, I, err…just received a call from Jardine."

I sat up in bed. "What? What did he say?"

"He apologised for doubting my friendship and then thanked me for looking after you while he wasn't here."

"Oh, I was going to call you in the morning and tell you."

"It's fine. But the way he spoke, I assumed you'd told him everything."

I held my breath, anticipating Oliver's next words.

"When he said *he,* meaning Ewan, I thought he knew, and I made a comment about keeping his friends in line. Next minute he was quizzing me and I had to tell him. I'm sorry, Ava, I didn't know."

"How did he react?" I whispered.

"He was quiet. But I explained that Ewan was off-his-face drunk and probably didn't remember. I tried to tone it down for your sake. Not that I think you should have to tone it down."

"Shit. He hasn't called me. God, I hope he doesn't do anything stupid." I checked the time. "It's after ten so he's probably asleep. I'll call him in the morning and talk to him."

"I'm sorry, Ava."

"It's fine, you didn't know. I wish now I'd told him, but I just couldn't at the time, you know?"

"I know. Remember, Ava, none of this is your fault. Whatever happens, it's not your fault."

"Thanks, Oliver. I appreciate you saying that. Do you have Ewan's number? I mean it's late to call, but..."

"Already tried. Went straight to voicemail."

"Damn. Well, I'll be talking to them both in the morning. God, Ewan probably can't remember a thing."

"Don't go alone. I'll come with you."

"Thanks. I'll give you the heads-up tomorrow."

After hanging up, I flopped back on the bed and checked for missed calls. I tapped on Jardine's name and waited. The dark room heightened my senses. The longer it took Jardine to pick up, the faster my heart began to beat. As soon as the call went to voicemail, I tried calling him again. This time I listened to the sound of his smooth voice.

"Jardine, I need to talk to you. I know you're probably asleep so call me in the morning. It's important. I love you."

I held my phone to my chest and prayed Jardine called back before confronting Ewan. Resolved to thinking Jardine was asleep, I rolled over and shut my eyes.

A half-hour later, my phone buzzed on my bedside table. I checked the screen. A private number. I silenced it and waited for the voicemail message to ding. As soon as I heard Ewan's voice, my heart sped up.

"Ava, I'm so sorry. I can't remember what happened last night, but I do remember seeing you outside the club. Jardine has been here yelling and threatening me. I don't know what the hell's going on. My dad called his, and his father came and calmed him down. I don't know what to say but 'I'm sorry.' I'll call you tomorrow."

Shit.

I tapped on Jardine's name. Ewan could wait.

No answer.

I sent Jardine a message.

Call me ASAP xx

Mr Kumble had to calm Jardine. Shit, this was bad. I tried calling Jardine again. Voicemail.

"Jardine, please call me. We need to talk."

I remained awake, clutching my phone, waiting for him to call. It was the last thing I remembered.

My eyes opened when I heard two knocks on my door. I rolled over and reached for my phone to check the time. It wasn't on the table. I sat up quickly, remembering how last night went down. I flipped the sheets, searching for it.

"Ava?" Mum's voice came from the other side of the door. "Are you awake?"

"Come in," I croaked.

I located my phone as Mum strolled into the room. "Jardine is here."

"What?" I patted my hair flat.

"He's in the living room. He doesn't look happy," Mum whispered.

"Send him in."

Mum frowned at me, stepped into my room and closed the door. She walked to the bed and sat on the edge. "Darling, what's going on with you two? If you want him to come back later—"

"No," I interrupted. "I want to see him now." I reached out and touched her hand. "Trust me."

Mum tilted her head. "Fine. I'll be in the kitchen if you need me."

As soon as the door closed, I scrolled through my phone, looking for a message or a missed call.... nothing. The door opened and Jardine stepped inside wearing my favourite chino cut-offs and a white polo. His gaze raked over me. Without caring about my bed hair or morning breath, I jumped out of bed and stood before him. For a moment, his stern expression mellowed when his gaze landed on the teddy on my nightdress. When his gaze lifted, the seriousness in his eyes had returned. I reached out and touched his hand, then slowly weaved my fingers with his. He didn't pull away but his fingers were limp, and he showed no effort to hold my hand. At this moment, I knew it was bad.

"I'm sorry," I whispered. My eyes pleaded with his.

For a few seconds, he didn't answer, simply staring at me as though I'd landed from Mars. "Me too," he finally said.

He stepped away from me and walked to the end of the bed, deliberately putting space between us. I held my breath...waiting.

"Why?"

I barely heard him.

I stepped closer. "Why?" I repeated. I struggled to breathe normally.

He strode to the window and opened the blinds, peering out at the front garden. "Why didn't you tell me?" He turned to me. His forehead crinkled as though in pain. "Why keep a secret? Why trust Oliver and not me?

"No." I went to him and took both his hands in mine. "It's not how it seems." I raised each hand and kissed his knuckles. I placed both his hands over my heart, on my breast. "My heart beats only for you. Please understand that. I know it was wrong not to tell you, but I was trying to protect us."

"Us?" His eyes narrowed. "How were you protecting *us* by lying to me? You have no idea the damage it's caused."

"No." I shook my head. I took his hands and wrapped them around my back, making him hold me. I released his hands, then placed my hands on his chest. He didn't move and yet he barely touched my back. Tears formed in my eyes, knowing how much I'd hurt him. "Please, Jardine. I'm sorry. I wanted to explain but didn't want to make everything even worse. Bringing up what happened already ruined last night. I didn't want you to be mad. Especially when I know you have to focus on cricket."

He looked away. "Now you sound like my father."

"What?" Oh God, his father. "What happened last night?"

He stepped away from me and glanced at the door. I didn't know if he wanted to yell but thought better of it, knowing my parents were not far away, or if he wanted to bolt.

"What do you think went down last night, Ava? That I visited Ewan and had a beer with him?" He pushed his hand over his head. "*Bas ab mere se nahi hoga.*"

My hands trembled. Jardine rarely spoke Hindi in front of me. "Did Ewan remember?"

"No. But he admitted he weas fucked up. What did you say to him?"

"Nothing. I swear he came to me, forced himself on me. Oliver said he told you."

"So you've talked to Oliver." It wasn't a question.

I nodded.

His gaze lowered and focused on the floor. He rubbed at the side of his neck. Seeing his expression, I wished I could read his mind.

"My father wanted me to come here and break up with you."

Air whooshed from me as a wrecking ball smashed into my chest. "What?"

His fists clenched at his side. "He said that you're distracting me from my purpose. Education and cricket come first. He thinks you're bringing out the worst in me."

I shook my head. Tears streamed down my cheeks. My heart sliced open, and I wanted to beg him not to listen to his father.

"He accused me of losing self-control, disgracing him and my Hindu beliefs." His chin dipped.

I closed the gap between us and threw my arms around his waist. "You were protecting me."

"No, I retaliated after what happened to you. Last night... I scared myself," he rasped. "I wanted to kill Ewan, despite him being a friend. The look on his face..." Jardine shook his head disbelievingly. "I don't know what came over me."

He wrapped his arms lightly around me, as though he was afraid to touch me...or forbidden.

I squeezed his middle and buried my head in his chest. "No. Your father doesn't know us. I can't live without you."

My words must have hit the right spot as Jardine then picked me up and dropped me in the centre of the bed. His body pressed into mine as he kissed me, long and hard. His hands snaked behind my neck, holding my face to his, kissing me as though it were the last. Tears trickled down my cheeks, hoping and praying it wasn't.

Bunching fists of hair in my hands, I kissed him with every ounce of love in my body. I opened my legs so he fell between my thighs. He broke the kiss and stared at me, wide-eyed. I knew what he was thinking...my parents were just on the other side of the door. "Take them off," I whispered. Seconds later, my panties fell to the floor and Jardine kicked off his cut-offs. I gasped, realising he had gone commando. For a second, I caught a glimpse of his erection before he was inside of me. I arched my back as relief coursed through my body, filling the void in my heart. With every thrust, emotion flowed from Jardine, enveloping my body entirely, piercing my soul. I ran my hands under his polo and over the small of his back, feeling his muscles work.

Jardine kissed his way to my neck, one hand slipping under my nightdress, massaging my breast. Unlike our nights in the hotel, I found my release quickly. My breath quickened and Jardine placed his hand lightly over my mouth. He trembled before driving himself into me one last time. His eyes glazed over and his head fell on the pillow next to mine. I wrapped my ankles around his thighs and tightened my arms over his back.

I turned my head and gazed into his beautiful eyes that were mere inches away from mine. His finger stroked my cheek. We savoured the minutes of holding each other close after making love until muffled voices from the kitchen startled us. Jardine dressed quickly.

"Wait while I shower?" I had to hold back from pleading.

His lips pressed into a thin line. "I have to go. Promised Dad I'd run a few errands. Gotta be responsible," he added. "But I'll come back around lunch."

"Wait." I grabbed his hand. "You said something before...in Hindi. What did you say?"

His gaze darted away from me.

I squeezed his hand. "Jardine. It's okay. Tell me."

His lips separated. I waited. "That's it, I can't do this anymore."

My shoulders sagged. "Were you talking about us, or about arguing with your father?" It hurt to ask, but I had to know.

He closed his eyes. "Everything. Us—my father—cricket—all that's expected of me." He opened his eyes and I caught a glimpse of the pain behind them.

"And now?"

He scooped up my hand from the bed and trailed his fingers to my shoulder, my skin tingling under his touch. His hand stopped over my left breast, cupping it as though holding my heart. "Even if my father ordered me to break up with you, I couldn't. Because part of me would always belong to you, and I'd never be able to be the best man possible if part of me were missing. The only way we'll break up is if you tell me to go. I don't have the strength. It would have to come from you."

I pulled him to my chest and held him, aching for him even though he was still here with me. "Then we'll always be together."

CHAPTER 9

Cleo's mum led me through the house to the pergola out back, where Cleo sat cross-legged in a chair, reading a magazine and sipping coffee.

"Hey," I said and leaned to kiss her cheek.

Cleo hugged me with her free hand. "Hey you. Wasn't expecting you 'til later. I have a list of places we can apply. Do you have anywhere in mind?"

Shit, I forgot about applying for work and writing résumés with Cleo. I could feign a response, but I'd learned my lesson yesterday. "I'm actually here for another reason." I sank into the seat beside her.

Cleo flipped the magazine shut. She gave me a sceptical look. "Okay…"

I bit my lip. There was no way to say it but to come right out with it. "I lied to you about Saturday night."

Cleo's eyes narrowed. "Which part?"

"About leaving the club early with Oliver because I was sick. And it's not what you think," I added after her brow arched. "Ewan forced himself on me."

"What?" she jerked back.

I raised my hand. "Let me get it all out first."

Cleo nodded and took a sip of coffee. "I've got a feeling we're going to need more than coffee when you're done."

By the time I finished telling Cleo about Ewan and how Jardine and his father reacted, she had tears trickling down her cheeks. She pulled me into a hug. "Why didn't you trust me enough to tell me? I'm your best friend. I would've been there for you."

"I know. I've hurt you and Jardine, the two people I care for most. I'm sorry." I leaned my forehead on her shoulder. "I want to confront Ewan. Oliver insists on coming, but I don't want Jardine there."

"He'll want to be there. I can imagine how lousy he's feeling about not being there to protect you."

I nodded. "I don't want him to get angry. He needs to focus on cricket. His father already wants him to stay away from me and anyone who distracts him from his purpose." I couldn't keep the hurt from my voice.

"Screw his father. It has nothing to do with him."

I shrugged. "He only wants the best for Jardine. So do I."

Cleo didn't say anything for a while.

"So when are you planning on meeting with Ewan?"

"Jardine leaves again on Wednesday, so then?"

"Have you spoken with Ewan?"

"No."

Cleo plucked her phone from the elastic around her hip and tapped on the screen.

"What are you doing?" I gasped.

Cleo raised a hand. "Trust me."

Cleo told Ewan she knew about the incident and that she, Oliver, and I would be paying him a visit on Wednesday. In the meantime, he wasn't to contact me. After agreeing to meet somewhere private, she ended the call.

"We're meeting him at a park at Brighton Beach on Wednesday at eleven o'clock. You can fill Oliver in on the details."

I nodded. My fingers went to my elbow. I didn't know whether to feel relieved or panicked. Cleo hit my hand away.

"You can do this. You'll have us there to back you up. You have to face Ewan, and I think it's better not to wait."

Jardine arrived after lunch and remained by my side all afternoon. We lazed on the lounge watching movies, holding hands, and canoodling. There was probably more kissing than movie watching, except when Mum popped in for a chat. Thankfully, she kept herself busy in her craft room quilting the majority of the time.

At four o'clock, Mum asked Jardine to stay for dinner.

"Thank you, but I'm hoping Ava will come to my house for dinner."

I stiffened. Neither of us had brought up Ewan, his father or our fight.

"Well, that will make an easy dinner for me," Mum said, oblivious to my reaction.

I gave Jardine a sceptical glance. He squeezed my hand and nodded. "Please," he mouthed.

As soon as Mum exited the room, I shook my head at Jardine. "I don't want to start a fight between you and your father."

"You won't. Besides, he doesn't get home 'til late. If you want to leave when he gets home, I'll take you."

I closed my eyes and my stomach tensed in warning. Jardine's lips grazed my neck. "Please." He feather-kissed his way to my lips. "Mum's been lonely lately and I think the two of you could be good friends."

Admittedly, I'd hoped to get know his mother better. Previous times at his house we'd only eaten dinner then hung out in Jardine's private entertainment room. After dinner, his mother had always made herself scarce and I'd been more interested in being with Jardine than getting to know her. Now, with our relationship heading into serious territory, I needed to make an effort. "Okay. But the moment your dad shows any rudeness toward me, I want to leave."

"Deal," he whispered before kissing me.

Jardine lived near the city in a beige, two-story, five-bedroom home. It seemed impossibly big for just the tree of them. We pulled up out front and Jardine clicked the remote. Black steel gates opened, allowing us to drive along the paved driveway, around a water feature and park near the front door.

My heart beat nervously, knowing how his father had reacted to him fighting with Ewan, insisting that he stay away from me. It upset me they thought I was a mere distraction and didn't take our relationship seriously, especially since I'd do anything to help Jardine reach his goals and dreams. After all, if it weren't for his support helping me study and calming me through my exams, I probably would have failed.

Jardine took my hand and led me through the huge, cedar wood double doors. Inside the foyer, I tilted my head and admired the gold and crystal provincial chandelier. An imposing and grandeur feature—worth more than my car—and my favourite of all the luxe décor.

He guided me into the all-white kitchen, where his mum sat reading a magazine. She looked up and smiled, her warm expression easing my nerves a little.

"Ava, I'm so glad you could make it." She walked around and hugged me lightly. She glanced at Jardine and then back at me, her expression a touch worried. "I'm sorry to hear what happened to you. Young men and alcohol…" She shook her head. "I also regret some of my decisions from my youth. Although it does not excuse Ewan of his inappropriate behaviour."

Jardine stiffened beside me. I squeezed his hand. "Thank you, Mariah. I appreciate your support."

She smiled at me, and yet I sensed her husband did not share her opinion. "I'm cooking korma and it won't be ready for another half-hour."

"Ava and I will be in the study. Just call us when it's ready." Jardine indicated for me to follow him.

"Um, I might stay here and help your Mum." I smiled at him. "I know you have some paperwork to complete."

"Ava's right. Best you finish your diet and training progress forms in your diary. You don't want your father questioning you when he arrives home."

Jardine scowled at his mother. "When have I ever not done what's required of me?"

Mariah stroked her son's arm. "Sweetheart, you're doing a marvellous job and I'm proud of you. But after last night, I think it's best to keep the peace. Let Ava and I have a chat. Promise we won't talk badly of you." She winked at me and I smiled.

I lifted onto my tiptoes and kissed his cheek. "Go."

Jardine gave his mother a sideways glance before kissing my forehead. "I won't be long."

"Can I get you something to drink?" Mariah's hand lingered on the door of the fridge.

"A water will be fine, thanks." I sat down at the table next to the place she had been reading a magazine.

"I think you deserve a scotch, Ava, but I don't want to be the one to introduce you to a bad habit." Her smile reached her blue eyes.

I understood how Mr Kumble had fallen for Mariah. Blonde-haired, blue-eyed, and a heart-shaped face with impeccable cheekbones, I imagined all the boys crushed on her when she was young. Her goddess-like, tanned body, even now was intimidating.

She placed a glass of water in front of me and took her original place at the table beside me. "Like Jardine, I assume you're relieved to have finished school." I nodded. "Do you intend to find work before university starts?"

I nodded and took a sip of water. "Yes. I'm not sure where. I'm sending out résumés this week."

"It will help fill your time while Jardine's away."

"Yes." Her support shocked me.

"I won't lie. Travelling takes a toll on any relationship, not just yours as a very young couple. I think you both need to sit down and talk about how you're going to make it work."

"You don't think I'm distracting him like Mr Kumble?" The question shocked me at how easily it left my mouth. Did she have a superpower to calm my nerves?

Mariah placed her hand delicately over mine. Maybe her nursing background gave her the power to soothe.

"Ajay reminds me of his father, Sanjay. Jardine is not like his father or his grandfather; he's more like his grandmother and me. His grandmother welcomed me into the family, although Sanjay showed reluctance like Ajay is toward you. Trust me when I say he'll come around. At the end of the day, Jardine's happiness is the most important thing to us."

I smiled. "I love your son and only want what's best for him. I understand how hard it'll be with him away, but we promised each other to follow our dreams, no matter what. And cricket has always been his dream, even before he met me."

She patted my hand. "His passion for cricket started as a little boy and was influenced by his grandfather. Both Ajay and Sanjay idolised Douglas Jardine, whom my son was named after." I nodded in understanding. "He was born in India. The English cricketer, that is."

My eyes widened. "I didn't know that."

She smiled and looked away, her eyes glazing over. "I remember the day Ajay named our son. All he talked about was this courageous, intelligent man who inspired loyalty in his teammates and focused on whatever task was given to him without allowing emotion to get in the way. He spoke of a hero leading the English team to victory and who took on the Australians using controversial tactics at the time. But that's why Ajay holds so much respect for him. He was a genius. And because Douglas Jardine had a career and played cricket, my husband believes our son can do the same." She shook her head. "Ajay believes our Jardine will one day be a doctor, but I'm afraid if he's going to have a future in cricket, his other dream of becoming a doctor has to be put on hold."

"So you don't think he'll study medicine?"

She shook her head slowly, watching my expression carefully. "I know you've planned this together. However, his selection into the Australian team will make it difficult. It's nice to have a plan B."

"He's going to make the team, isn't he?" I managed.

Mariah genuinely looked sorry for me. "Yes."

In a deliberate attempt to change the subject, Mariah flicked open the magazine and pointed out a ball gown on a film star she admired.

"I have a gala for a hospital fundraiser and thought about a gown similar to this. Do you like it?"

I smiled half-heartedly. "It's stunning. And I think you'll look fabulous in it."

She gave me a gentle smile. "You don't think the gold fabric will make me look pale with my hair?"

"No." I couldn't imagine anything looking bad on her.

Jardine soon joined us and we chatted about topics that had nothing to do with cricket or the future. Current reality shows dominated the conversation, specifically the pros and cons of being a contestant. The three of us ate dinner and I temporarily forgot about Mr Kumble until I glanced up to find him standing in the dining room doorway.

"Evening," he said tersely, then placed his briefcase in the corner. "That was a day I'd rather forget."

"Ajay." Mariah pushed up from the table and walked to him. She kissed him on the cheek. "Can I get you some wine, love?"

"Yes, thank you." When Mariah disappeared, his gaze fell on me. "Hello, Jardine. Ava. I'm surprised to see you here."

I cringed and leaned closer to Jardine.

Jardine's hand went to my thigh. "Ava is my girlfriend, so I don't know why you're surprised."

"After last night—"

"Don't," Jardine snapped. "I'm not about to discuss it with you. My relationship with Ava is none of your business."

Mr Kumble's brow furrowed. "You're my business. I expect you to do the right thing, even if it means sacrificing pleasures in life, like Dada Jee and I did." His voice remained low and deep.

Jardine pushed his chair back and stood. "I'm not sacrificing my relationship with Ava, if that's what you're getting at."

"Jardine, please." I pulled at his hand. "I don't want you to fight with your father."

Mr Kumble replied in Hindi, and although he never raised his voice, I knew his words had offended Jardine by the way he stiffened beside me.

"*Haanji,*" Jardine replied. My heart raced as panic clawed at my throat.

More words were exchanged in Hindi. I recognised a few that Jardine had used before. Then I heard him say *biwi,* which translated to 'wife.' I assumed he was talking about his mother, but when Mr Kumble's demeanour cracked, his face reddening, I realised what Jardine had suggested. We loved each other, but for him to tell his father he wanted to marry me…well, I didn't want to be here for his reaction. Hearing Jardine say *biwi* out loud to his father scared me.

"*Yeh meri zindagi Hai,*" Jardine warned. He grabbed my hand. "I'm taking Ava home."

At that moment, Mariah entered the room. "What is going on, Ajay?"

"I told Dad to stay out of my life." Jardine looked down at me. "I'm sorry you had to witness our disagreement. But I don't want to stay here while my father is in a mood."

"A mood," his father echoed. "Jardine, a young man around your age suffered a heart attack and died while I was performing surgery on him today. I am not in a mood."

Mariah rubbed Mr Kumble's arm as she handed him a crystal glass filled with white wine. "Sweetheart. Sit down. Eat. Relax. You'll feel better." She turned to face Jardine. "I'm sure your father didn't mean—"

"You didn't hear what he said about Ava. I'm taking her home."

Mariah turned to Mr Kumble. "Honey?"

His lips pressed tight. "I thinks it's best if Ava leaves." He turned to me. "I didn't mean to offend you, Ava. I'm looking out for my son, as any father would."

Jardine made a gruff noise before leading me toward the door. I turned to Mariah. "Thank you for dinner. I hope I can see you soon." Then I set my disapproving gaze on Mr Kumble. "I hope you have a better evening, sir."

Jardine never spoke a word until we pulled up in front of my house.

He killed the engine and stared at the road ahead. "I'm sorry you had to witness that."

I reached over and touched his hand that rested on the gear stick. "I have no idea what was said, but from your reaction, I gather your father insulted me."

Jardine glanced down at my hand covering his. He took my hand in both of his before looking up to meet my gaze.

"Your father loves you and is only looking out for you. I get that."

He looked at me disbelievingly. "I don't deserve you."

"He thinks I'm not good enough for you, doesn't he?"

Jardine's nostrils flared. "I don't want to talk about him."

"Jardine." I scrambled closer to touch him. "I deserve to know what he said. I want to know where I stand."

"You stand with me...beside me." His voice sounded strained.

I stroked his cheek, my hand lingering. "What did he say that upset you?"

My heart ached seeing the tears in his eyes.

"He thinks you're a fling and as soon as I'm away with cricket, I'll forget about you. That while we're having sex, I'm distracted. He thinks you could ruin me and convince me not to play. He also accused you of possibly getting pregnant and forcing me to give up everything I've dreamed of. I told him if you were, I'd be happy and marry you."

"What?" I gasped. I couldn't help the tears welling, but I quickly swiped them away. What did I do for his father to think so low of me? "We promised to help each other follow our dreams. I'm so proud to think you're close to reaching yours."

Jardine trapped a tear with his finger. "But I also dreamed of going to university with you," he said.

I shook my head. "You wanted the cricket dream more."

Jardine reached for me and pulled me into his chest. We remained still, simply holding each other, knowing time was running out. Jardine's phone vibrated in the console with an incoming message. He swiped the screen, saying it was from his mum.

He stared at the screen longer than normal before looking at me with an apologetic gaze. "Dad just received a phone call informing me of my selection to the Australian team. He thinks I should go home and return the call."

I smiled broadly and threw my arms around his neck. "Congratulations, babe. I knew you'd do it!"

He coughed and laughed together. He shook his head. "Yeah, I can't believe it, but I did." Then he gave me a celebratory kiss.

And yet I couldn't help feeling as if I'd just lost.

CHAPTER 10

In a whirlwind of emotion, I watched Jardine pack his bags. Upon returning the call to the Australian cricket team, he learned that he needed to attend a training camp with the squad and then be available for the Test series against India in Melbourne the following weekend.

Lying on my stomach on his bed, I pushed up onto my elbows. "You'll be playing against India. Is that weird for you?"

"Not weird, more euphoric. To think my first international game will be against my grandfather's team, it's like…" he paused, staring at me for a second before joining me on the bed, "a dream. One you helped me achieve."

I smiled, knowing it didn't reach my eyes. "I didn't do anything. It was all you."

Jardine stretched out next to me and pulled me onto him. "I'm a better person because of you. Knowing that if I fail, you'll be there, no matter what. It makes the challenge less of a risk, if you know what I mean."

My heart swelled with adoration. "I'm proud of you."

He stroked my hair, winding strands around his fingers. "I've been thinking. The weekend after next when I'm in Melbourne, I want you to come watch me play. It will mean a lot, knowing my parents and my girlfriend will be watching my first game."

I gave a little squeal. Then I groaned, realising financially it wasn't a possibility. "I want to, but I don't have any money."

"Ava." He frowned at me. "I'll pay and don't argue. I want you there, so it's my treat." He rolled over and snagged his iPad from the floor. I watched as he typed in Webjet on Google.

"Jardine. I have to check with my parents." My stomach cartwheeled, thrilled yet apprehensive.

He glanced sideways at me. "We're eighteen and no longer in school. I'm paying, so I don't see how they can say anything."

My parents still treated me as though I was sixteen. "Maybe."

"You're coming to Melbourne. Send Cleo a text and see if she wants to come, and I'll pay for her as well. It won't cost me any extra for your room."

It dawned on me that if Cleo were in the room with me, I wouldn't see much of Jardine. "Will I see you?"

"Not as much as I'd like. There'll be some time after the game, but I suspect I won't be able to leave the team. It would mean a lot to me if you were there though." He kissed my cheek.

I stalled a moment. "What if I fly over for the day? Arrive early and leave on the last flight home, since I can't spend the night with you. That way my parents will stress less."

He gave me a long look. "Deal."

He typed in my personal details. After a few minutes, he grinned. "I just forwarded you the confirmation email. Now..." he pulled me close and kissed my ear, "let me show you how I want to fill in the next hour."

Wednesday was sure to be the worst day of the year. Not only did Jardine fly out early this morning, I'd arranged to meet with Ewan and talk about "the incident." With so many emotions circling my brain, any rational thoughts rapidly turned to mush. Everything I touched, I'd drop, and not without Mum noticing and commenting.

Oliver picked me up at noon to go meet Cleo and Ewan at the park by the beach. We pulled into a car park next to Cleo's yellow Astra. I glanced down at my hands trembling in my lap. Oliver reached over and squeezed my hands. "Hey, it's going to be okay."

"Easy for you to say." I couldn't help feeling vulnerable with Jardine gone.

"You're stronger than this," Oliver reminded me. Then he frowned as his gaze focused on something or someone in front of the car.

I followed his gaze to two people standing near the swings in the park. Cleo stood in front of Ewan, jabbing a finger at his chest. "Shit." I jumped from the car, hearing Oliver's car door slam immediately after mine. Knowing he had my back, I stormed toward Ewan and Cleo.

Ewan turned and caught sight of us. He strode toward me with Cleo breaking into a trot to keep up. Ewan stopped a few feet away and Oliver jumped in front of him.

"Mate," he said to Oliver. "Give me some credit. I'd never intentionally do anything to hurt Ava."

"Maybe not intentionally, but you already have, idiot," Oliver spat. Then he stepped aside and my eyes locked with Ewan's.

"I'm so fucking sorry. I had no idea. You've got to believe me," he pleaded. "I'd never act like a douchebag if I wasn't so fucked up."

Cleo folded her arms over her chest. "He admitted to taking ecstasy," she said in a disgusted tone.

I shook my head. "Do you know the problems you caused in Jardine's family?"

He rubbed his hands up and down his face. "Yeah, I do. I stuffed up."

"I don't think he'll speak to you for a while."

Ewan put his hands low on his hips and tilted his head back to stare at the sky. "You're not telling me anything I don't know."

"Wait a minute." Oliver stepped closer. "Ava, this is not about Ewan's friendship with Jardine. It's about him apologising to you and giving you the respect you deserve."

"I do, mate, I do," Ewan reiterated. Then he faced me. "Ava, I don't know how to say anything other than I'm sorry, and I promise it will never happen again."

"Damn right," Cleo said in a low voice.

"I know it's going to take a while for you to trust me, but I'm not *that* guy."

"Well, do yourself a favour and stay off the drugs," Cleo snarled.

I folded my arms. "And Ewan… I'm not a slut."

"I've never thought of you that way," he said quickly. His eyes darted to Oliver, then back to me. "Serious."

I gave a quick nod, though I wasn't altogether convinced. "I forgive you, and maybe I'll trust you again one day. Until then, you'll have to earn it." I massaged the knot in the back of my neck. Turning to Oliver, I said, "I've had enough for one day." Then I headed in the direction of the car.

"I'm proud of you," Oliver said as he kept in step with me. "You're stronger than you give yourself credit for."

"I don't feel strong. I feel like shit."

"Because he's gone away?"

I nodded. Just then, Cleo caught up with us. "Want some company?"

I stopped in front of the car. "I won't be any fun today. Think I'll go home… and cry myself to sleep."

"Like hell. I'm not letting you go home and wallow, Ava. We'll do the résumés like we planned."

"You both looking for work?" Oliver glanced from Cleo to me.

"Yeah. Over the holidays." I need money, and it would help fill in time with Jardine not around.

Oliver grinned. "My dad is looking for waitresses at our restaurant. Call in this afternoon and talk to him. You know I'll put in a good word."

"The three of us working together over the holidays? That would be sick," Cleo said excitedly.

I smiled at her. "We'll be working, not partying," I reminded her. "Okay. I'm going home first. You talk with your dad and if he's interested in hiring us, give me a call." I glanced at Cleo's long legs in denim shorts. We both needed to change.

As soon as I stepped into the house, I wanted to collapse on the lounge. Instead, Mum greeted me with a smile from ear to ear.

"We've had the best news, Ava." She paused and I seriously hoped she didn't expect me to guess. My first response would be to ask if Jardine had come home. Because that's the only news I wanted to hear.

"Your Aunt Margaret called your father this morning and she invited us to holiday in St. Louis."

I shook my head, not comprehending.

"You remember your aunt, don't you? Oh maybe not, but we've shown you photographs."

"The aunt that visited when I was six?"

"Yes." Mum led me into the kitchen. "We're going to have a white Christmas because after meeting her in St Louis, she's paying for us to go to New York!" Mum made an exaggerated happy face. "Oh Ava, we're going to have the best time."

I stared at my mother. My stomach plummeted to the ground. "But Jardine will be home for Christmas and New Year's. I'll hardly see him."

Mum tilted her head at me. "Ava, really? We're about to go on our first overseas trip as a family and you're worried about not seeing Jardine? There'll be other times for you to see him, but this holiday is a great opportunity to see relatives we haven't seen in years."

I shut my eyes tight, trying to block out my mother and the rest of the world.

"Ava?"

I opened my eyes and wiped away the wetness. "I've got hay fever." I blew my nose into a tissue. "Sorry. It's great news, Mum," I said in my fake-happy voice. "But I need to lie down a while."

Mum didn't say anything, although her look told me she wasn't convinced I was suffering from allergies.

Today had officially turned into the worst day ever.

Two hours later, I woke from a nap at the sound of my cell phone. My vision blurred and I concentrated on focusing when Jardine's name appeared on the screen.

"Hi," I said, trying to sound awake-ish.

"Hi, babe." His smooth voice caressed me.

"So you arrived safely?" I forced a neutral tone, hiding the pent-up emotion brewing inside of me.

"And unpacked... I miss you already."

That's all it took for the tears to flow. "I miss you too. So much it hurts."

Silence fell for a few seconds and I swiped away the tears, glad he couldn't see me. For Christ's sake, it was only the first day.

"Are you crying, Ava?"

"No," I croaked.

"Ava, I know when you're crying. Did something happen?"

"No. Yes." Nothing...yet everything. "I sorted things out with Ewan today." I heard him suck in a breath, so I continued before he jumped to conclusions. "We're okay for now. And I might have work at Oliver's family's restaurant. With Cleo. So that should pass the time while you're gone." He remained silent as though digesting my words. "I miss you."

"Babe. I know it's hard, but think of every day passing as one closer to us being together again. My instinct is to think of you every minute of the day, but I can't allow myself. Otherwise, I'll cave. We have to be strong for each other."

I nodded. "I'm just having a bad day. Probably PMS, you know."

"Yeah. I know," he joked. "So you, Cleo and Oliver get to spend the summer working together. I know I should be happy, but I can't help feeling jealous."

I snorted. "Oh, 'cause I'll be having so much fun waitressing in the heat."

"I love you, babe. Never forget it. Look at your wrist and remember it's for a short time and we'll soon be together."

I turned my wrist and stared at the tattoo, the message connecting us. "And I will always love you."

"I'll try and call every day. But if not, I'll text you."

"It's fine, I understand. Bye, Jardine."

I didn't tell him about Christmas. He didn't need to know yet that my parents were going to drag me away from him to the other side of the world, stealing our precious time. Jardine's first priority was cricket and I didn't want to do or say anything to upset him—or his father.

CHAPTER 11

The days seemed longer with Jardine not around.

Every morning for the past nine days, I woke to *I love you* texts, which I assumed Jardine sent before his early-morning training sessions.

The good news is Mr Lombardi had agreed to hire Cleo and me as waitresses at his Italian restaurant over the summer. Somehow I didn't think Oliver gave him a choice. I knew it was my friend's way of keeping an eye on me and making sure I didn't remain at home, wallowing.

Last Sunday, Dad gave me 'the talk' about his expectations and how Jardine shouldn't be influencing my decisions when it concerned my life. I assumed Mum had mentioned my reaction to our family holiday. I wanted to argue that Jardine *was* my life but didn't want to upset him before church.

Dad printed copies of the dates of our flights and the itinerary for Christmas. We were to fly out on the twenty-second of December to St. Louis and spend a few days there before flying to New York for the New Year's festivities. Afterward, we'd fly back to St. Louis for a couple of days, then onto Los Angeles before arriving home on the seventh of January. I prayed Jardine would still be on Christmas break, but if he played well in the Test series in Melbourne this weekend, then the prospect of that happening would be unlikely.

I scratched at my elbow as I thought of the long international flight that scared the crap out of me. Grabbing my car keys, I pushed out any negative thoughts because I was finally going to see Jardine tomorrow.

So after my doctor appointment in half an hour, I intended to come home and pack. On my to-do list was another prescription for the pill and a general check-up. I'd been feeling lightheaded and nauseous the past few days, though I suspected the change of weather and emotional stress had contributed. I'd only been taking contraceptive pills the last eight months and was considering not taking them if Jardine and I were to be apart. We could just use condoms.

Another thing to discuss with my doctor.

Inside the waiting room, I picked up a newspaper and turned to the sports section. I read in bold letters:

Jardine Kumble Selected To Play Against India.

I smiled, pride filling me. Until I read on and irritation surfaced at the journalist who tried to make it controversial by mentioning his grandfather, Sanjay Kumble. They pointed out how he had played for India, yet Jardine was named after the English cricketer, Douglas Jardine.

When the nurse called my name, I folded the newspaper and attempted to calm myself. My blood pressure would probably be high. Dr Fairlow greeted me and closed the door behind me.

"Ava. What can I do for you?" She swivelled her chair to face me.

"Well, I need another script for the pill."

Dr Fairlow nodded and grabbed the cuff to the blood pressure machine. She mentioned the usual about blood clots and other things I'd heard before as she measured my blood pressure. We both stopped talking for a few moments.

"It's lower than usual," she stated. "Do you feel unwell at all?"

"Not really. I've had some nausea and dizziness, but I've been rather emotional lately with exams, finishing school... and other things. I put it down to PMS."

She nodded and documented my words. "Any burning when you pass urine?" She reached for a small container with a yellow screw-top lid and pulled it from the shelf.

"No. Not that I remember."

She smiled. "If you had a UTI—a urinary tract infection—you would remember. They're not pleasant." She handed me the container. "Can you pee into this?"

I nodded and walked out to find the restrooms. A few minutes later, I returned with the small container. Dr Fairlow took it to the sink and dipped different sticks in it. "This will take a few minutes." After washing her hands, she sat back down in the chair. "You're still sexually active?"

"Yes." I blushed.

"Do you use condoms?"

"No. I have a boyfriend, so..."

"He doesn't sleep around?"

My eyes rounded. "No," I said louder than necessary. "Why? Do you think I have an STD?"

"No, Ava. I'm not suggesting anything, just gathering information."

"Oh. Should I use condoms as well?"

She stood from her chair lend walked to the sink to check the sticks. "I always recommend condoms to prevent diseases, and because the pill is not one hundred percent effective."

"Oh."

Dr Fairlow approached me, carrying one stick in her hand. "Are you and your boyfriend close?"

"Yes," I whispered. My insides clenched, fearing she was going to tell me I had an STD, which could only mean one thing. No. I pushed the thought out. Not possible.

"Well, you're pregnant, Ava."

"What?" My head spun. *No, I couldn't be.* Suddenly, all the air was sucked out of the room and I had trouble breathing.

"Ava. Breathe," Dr Fairlow instructed.

I took a few deep breaths and leaned forward, head over my knees.

"Ava, sit back in the chair and lock your fingers behind your head. Close your eyes and concentrate on breathing, slow and deep." I did as she said.

The next few months flashed through my head. Summer with my friends. University. Jardine playing cricket in different countries. My family's vacation to America. Me, alone. And pregnant...

"Are you sure?" I managed.

Dr Fairlow held up the stick for me to see the plus sign. "You'll need a blood test to confirm your pregnancy and a due date. You might want to talk to someone, particularly your boyfriend. You can come and see me for your next ultrasound and then I'll refer you to an obstetrician."

My world tilted. I covered my face with my hands and burst into tears. Dr Fairlow patted my back. "I can write a referral for you to talk to a counsellor if you like." I didn't say anything. I just sobbed. "Ava. I think you should call a friend. Your blood pressure is already low, and you shouldn't drive alone while you're this upset. What about your boyfriend?"

I shook my head. "He's away...will be for a while," I mumbled, wiping my nose with my hands.

Dr Fairlow handed me a box of tissues. "A friend? Your parents?"

I blew my nose—hard. "Not my parents." I located Cleo's number in my phone and handed it to the doctor.

"Cleo? I'm Dr Fairlow, Ava's doctor."

"Yes, everything's fine."

Easy for her to say.

"Ava is not feeling well, and she would like you to meet her here at my practice. Could you drive her car home?"

"Thank you. She'll be waiting in the nurse's office."

She gave directions before handing back my phone. "Come with me to the nurse and she can take a blood test. She also has some pamphlets you can take home and read. By then, your friend should be here."

"Shut. Up." Cleo stared at me like I'd grown two heads. She started the engine and drove along at a snail's pace. I'd hardly said a word since she arrived. The nurse and Dr Fairlow had filled in the blanks.

"Now what?" I murmured. My thoughts had turned to mush and I couldn't think straight.

Cleo turned the corner and continued along the street at twenty kilometres an hour. "You have to tell him. Wait. Are you going to keep it?"

I stared at her, dumbfounded. Her words repeated in my brain. *Was I?*

I blinked, realising I had options. Bile rose at the back of my mouth. I stared at Cleo. "Yes."

"Holy fuck." She reached out and touched my arm. "When will you tell him? Tomorrow?"

I gaped at her. *Tomorrow.*

Shit. Tomorrow was his first international game...his big day. I shook my head. "No. Not tomorrow."

"Your parents?"

"No."

I stared out the window, dazed. I tried to imagine how Jardine might react. Elated probably, demanding we get married and live happily ever after? I huffed. Over his father's dead body. I remembered Mr Kumble's warning to Jardine, that I was merely a fling who'd fall pregnant and make Jardine give up his dream.

My stomach clenched. "I think I'm going to puke." I opened the window and breathed deeply.

"Do you want me to pull over?"

"No. I'll be all right in a minute. Just take me home. I still need to pack."

Cleo shot me a sideways glance. "So you're still going to see him but not tell him about the baby?"

"Yes. I'll wait for a couple of weeks until he comes home. Besides," I said, thinking more rationally, "The blood test might prove the urine test wrong."

Melbourne was one of my favourite cities, with its trendy cafes and fine restaurants. I walked along the city streets, noting the heavier traffic compared to Adelaide. I daydreamed about shopping here, taking in every storefront as I passed by, wishing I had more money to play with. At least it helped take my mind off... everything.

Last night I avoided all conversation with my parents, excusing myself to bed after dinner because of my early flight. It gave me time to ponder, to accept that I could be pregnant and consider the life choices—and sacrifices—I needed to make.

From the moment I woke this morning, I had butterflies about seeing Jardine, and the fluttering remained even now as I walked toward the Melbourne cricket oval.

The crowd thickened as I approached the gate. I pulled out my phone and read Jardine's text again.

Go to southern gate member's ticket booth. Your ticket will be there with your name on it. Not sure of procedure after the game. I'll text you ASAP. Hopefully, we can meet out for dinner. I love you xx

After collecting my ticket, I walked robotically toward the stadium seating. The grandstands filled quickly with the estimated 90,000 fans expected to attend today. Unlike my previous experience at the gentleman's game, I'd dressed up for the occasion in a black knee-length skirt, a pink blouse and black heels. I found a seat among strangers. I smiled at the lady beside me and a young boy on the other side. I twisted in my seat, taking in the anonymous faces around me, searching for Jardine's parents. My gaze lifted to a corporate area with seats behind a glassed window. My shoulders relaxed, since I assumed Mr Kumble would be in the most expensive seats.

The crowd roared and I turned my head to see a line of men dressed in white as they strolled onto the field. I craned my neck, searching for Jardine. I found him at the back of the line, head held high, taking in the atmosphere and the crowd. Green and yellow flags waved madly from the stands, dominating the blue of India.

"You missed the toss, dear," the lady next to me said. "India won the toss and elected to bat first. Australia will field."

"Thank you."

The crowd settled when an Australian lined up, ready to bowl. The first bowler was a pace bowler and he finished the over without a wicket. The second bowler didn't have a long run-up, so I knew he was a spin bowler. Jardine mentioned that spin bowlers were skilful and smart in the way they delivered the ball to the batsman. The spin on the ball caused the batter to swing and misjudge the delivery, leading to being bowled out. Or if they hit the ball awkwardly, caught out. Despite a few gasps from the crowd he also finished the over without a wicket. Jardine lined up to bowl next. I heard a few people around me making comments about "the rookie."

I held my breath and crossed my fingers, praying for Jardine to do well. He walked a long way back from the pitch, then rubbed the ball, spun it in the air and caught it. Then he took off, building up speed as he ran toward the pitch. He leapt into the air, landed, and hurled the ball toward the batsman at lightning speed. The Indian batsman swung and missed. The ball struck the wickets.

Holy fuck!

Jardine clean bowled the batter on his first ball. The crowd roared and cheered. Players from around the oval sprinted toward Jardine and jumped on him, ruffling his hair and patting his back.

My heart swelled and pride warmed me to my core, knowing what he was feeling behind his big smile. A single tear of joy trickled down my cheek. It was a magical moment and something I'd remember for years to come.

I settled back in my seat when the next batsman took the field. Jardine walked to the same spot, rubbed the ball on his pants, tossed it in the air twice, then took off, building speed like a cheetah running down its prey—only the prey was an Indian batsman. Jardine leapt into the air with a little skip before propelling another ball at the wicket. The batsman blocked the ball, but it hurled off the bat at a funny angle. Jardine dove, arms reaching out in front to catch the ball.

He landed and raised his arm with the ball in his hand. I shook my head in disbelief. Jardine had taken his second wicket on his second ball. Surely this was some kind of record, especially since he's only eighteen. The crowd applauded, chants taking over the screams. "Jar-dine, Jar-dine, Jar-dine."

Pride, joy, and relief rocked me as the players once again ran to him. I turned to the big screen in time to see the camera zooming in on his beautiful face. I stared at his image, larger than life.

At that moment, a part of my heart cracked, knowing Jardine had found his destiny. I now understood his father's words when he said that Jardine's future didn't include me.

For the remainder of the game, I savoured every moment, wanting to keep the memory with me forever. As the day's game drew to a close, I knew this would be one of the last times I'd see him. No way would the Australian team drop him from the squad now. Jardine was unique, and I knew that better than anyone.

I could feel myself sinking into sadness with every wicket he took, as if a burst of wind in his sails was sending him further away from me.

Jardine ended up with four wickets for the day. I waited for the crowd to thin out before I attempted to exit out of the gates. I imagined the celebrations in the locker rooms, the excitement that his teammates and parents would get to share with him. I wanted to tell security who I was and go to him, but I expected they wouldn't believe me.

Instead, I followed the crowd down a busy street and to the restaurants at Southbank. I wandered inside a steak and seafood restaurant and asked for a table for two, hoping there might be a chance Jardine could join me soon. My flight home wasn't until nine o'clock, so I'd need to catch a cab around seven-thirty. That left two hours to sit here and hope that he'd find me.

Jardine

I pulled out my phone and sent a message.

Great game today, babe. So proud of you. The crowd adored you. Glad I was here to watch. I'm at Leo's restaurant on Southbank. Will be here until 7.30. Hope I can see you. I love you xxxxx

An hour passed and I received no messages. I finally ordered a steak because after reading in a health pamphlet the doctor gave me the importance of keeping up iron levels. The longer I sat alone, the more melancholic my mood turned, believing this would be my life now.

Maybe the baby was my destiny, as cricket was Jardine's. We promised each other we would always be together, and in one way, Jardine would always be a part of me. My heart fluttered, thinking of how I would share my news with him, but just as quickly my stomach churned when I imagined his father's reaction.

I couldn't bring myself to admit his father was right. I could see myself fading into the background as the one-time fling of the famous cricket player. I could tell him I was pregnant, knowing that he'd choose me, or set him free to live his dream as we'd both originally planned.

When I glanced at the clock it read *seven-ten.* I didn't see the point of remaining here alone. I paid for my meal and headed out front toward a line of yellow taxis. Just as my hand went to the door handle, I heard my name being shouted behind me.

"Ava!"

I spun around, relieved at the sound of his voice.

"Jardine, you made it." My heart sped up. He grabbed me and spun me away from the taxi and into his arms. "My phone died. I'm sorry." He didn't wait for a response. He kissed me, his thumbs scooting along my jawline to the back of my neck. The intensity of the kiss surprised me. My hands resting on his hips, I stepped closer and we melted together.

"Oh my God, you were sensational today, " I said when we finally came up for air.

"Shut up and kiss me." His hands held onto my face, savouring every second we had together.

"What took you so long?" I gasped.

"Formalities. I was hoping you'd be there after the game with my parents."

"I didn't know where to go or what to do," I admitted.

He led me away to the side of the restaurant, then pulled me into his arms and hugged me like he was afraid of losing me. "I've missed you so much."

"I've missed you too."

"I'll be back at the beginning of December for a week, then gone until the twenty-first. I'll be home for Christmas." He smiled at me as though it were the best news he could have possibly shared.

My chin dipped. His finger lifted my face until my gaze met his. "What? I thought that would make you happy?"

I nodded. "It does, except I won't be home for Christmas. My aunt who lives in America has invited my family to stay. My father is excited about the prospect of a white Christmas."

His expression drooped. "When do you leave?"

"The twenty-second of December, arriving back on the sixth of January." I cursed at the tears welling in my eyes. At least now I knew why I'd been emotional.

"We'll only get one night together before I'm gone for a month?" His eyes searched mine, desperately looking for another answer.

We had no answers. This was fate. It was meant to be.

Que Sera.

"I know. Things are going to be difficult between us." I could feel the pain of separation already affecting us. "Maybe this is how it's meant to be..."

"What? What are you saying?" His brow crinkled.

"Maybe we should—"

"No." He placed his fingers on my lips. A look of horror crossed his face. "You can't destroy one of the best days of my life, Ava."

"I'm trying to do what's best for you." I snuggled into his chest. "I love you. I'll always love you."

He kissed the top of my hair. "It's killing me being away from you. But we can do this. We *have* to do this. I can't let you walk away from me just because we have to spend some time apart."

"Okay," I whispered, and Jardine didn't waste a moment before he kissed me again. I couldn't move. Drenched in the passion from his lips, I momentarily forgot all my problems.

"I'll see you in early December," he promised. "I love you."

"I'll be waiting."

CHAPTER 12

Only two other people shared my secret: Cleo and Oliver.

I'd managed to get through all of November without my parents suspecting anything. During the day, I watched movies in my room and nibbled on Salada biscuits to help with the morning sickness. At night, if not working, I'd visit Cleo.

Should I tell him? Should I not tell him? It was an internal battle eating away at me. Oliver and Cleo sided to convince me to tell Jardine. "If it were me, I'd want to know," Oliver had said.

In my heart, I knew what Oliver was saying. Jardine would be the perfect father, a doting lover, and a devoted partner. I knew if he had the choice, he'd choose me. Jardine would want to be by my side. He'd forgo his dream, giving it all up for his baby and me.

But could I do that to him?

No.

I loved him too much. So the kindest way to let him off the hook was to not tell him. But to give him his dream, it meant breaking up and maybe not seeing him again. Because if Jardine ever found out I'd deceived him and kept our child a secret, the fallout would destroy us both.

A decision needed to be made. When I thought about giving Jardine the future he dreamed about, it made sense and I convinced myself I could do it—for him. But it was easier in my head because when I processed it, my heart ached and the nausea increased tenfold. My hands trembled, thinking about a future without him, and the gut-wrenching pain scared me. I'd never be whole, losing the part of me that belonged to him. Thinking about the future stressed me out so I blocked those thoughts as best as I could and lived each day, waiting for his visit.

The night before Jardine was due to return home, I agreed to work. After tonight, I'd have a week with Jardine to myself...a week to decide my future.

"So you can cover for me?" I confirmed with Cleo as we swept and mopped the floors after closing.

"She can," Oliver interrupted. "And if you need more time off after, just call."

"I have the perfect boss," I admitted.

Oliver winked at me. "I'm serious. With Jardine home, I know you'll need the extra time to… talk."

"Thank you."

After locking up and saying goodbye to Cleo and Oliver, I headed to my car. A white Mercedes parked behind my car caught my eye. When the car door opened and Jardine stepped out, my knees almost gave way.

He ran to me, pulled me into his arms and kissed me. I relished his lips on mine, warm, soft and needy. His tongue sucked and licked playfully, reminding me how he could easily make me fall apart. "You came home early," I said against his lips.

"Couldn't stay away another day." He straightened and pulled me into his chest. "What are the chances I can sleep at yours tonight?"

"Zero unless you sleep on the lounge."

"Then come back to mine. Send a message that you're sleeping at Cleo's." He touched my cheek with the back of his hand. "My parents are away until Tuesday. Dad has an interview at a hospital in Sydney."

"Your parents are moving?"

He shrugged. "Maybe."

I didn't want to waste time thinking about his parents. "I don't have a change of clothes."

Jardine grinned. "Exactly."

Hundreds of butterflies took flight in my stomach. I didn't hesitate sending a text to Mum and then to Cleo, informing her of my plan.

I followed him to his house in my car. With a time bomb now ticking inside me, I studied him while he unlocked the front door, memorising every little detail I'd taken for granted in the past. "There's something different about you. You've cut your hair."

He gave me a sideways glance and grinned. "I have. Do you like it?"

"I do." I couldn't take my eyes off of him. He looked... older. "So... how's Melbourne?"

"It's okay. The guys are great. They look out for me." He pushed open the door and an unusual aroma hit me.

"What's that smell?"

"Mum burned some *diyas* before she left. She and my Dad still celebrate some Hindu festivals."

I walked through the foyer. A newly framed print of a decorated elephant caught my eye. Candles on plates sat on a side table.

Walking up the stairs to his bedroom, his house seemed eerily quiet and dark. A big, empty home gave me the jitters.

His bedroom appeared untouched from the last time I was here, meticulously clean and not a thing out of place except a suitcase in the corner. "Is your mum now Hindu?" Not sure why I wanted to know, but I couldn't help but wonder… if I practiced Hindu, would his father accept me?

He shook his head. "But she celebrates at certain times with Dad and thinks some of the deities make sense. She's all about free love, but I think she mainly likes the festivities."

"What about you? Do you practice alone now, and not because your father makes you?" I pushed loose strands of hair back into my knotted bun.

Jardine opened his mouth to speak, then his expression softened and he changed his mind. "You're my religion. I worship the body I dream about…" He reached me in two short steps. His hands trailed down my shoulders to my breasts and landed on my hips. In a quick action, he pulled me against him and I could feel him hard against my thigh. I smiled at him. "I can get down on my knees if you don't believe me," he offered. He bent on one knee and slid his hands under the elastic of my skirt.

I stopped him from sliding it down. "Okay, I believe you. Do you mind if I shower first?"

He considered it a moment. "As long as I can wash your back… among other things."

I didn't need any coaxing. I took his hand and led him to his ensuite. He slowly unbuttoned my shirt and slid it over my arms. My skin tingled at the slightest brush with his. Then he pulled the black skirt down my hips and my legs, along with my panties. He lingered a moment on his knees, kissing my bare thighs. My hands trembled like a drug addict about to inject the next fix. I curled my fingers into his hair, feeling his warm breath on my sensitive skin. He stood and unclipped my bra and watched me carefully as the straps fell over my arms and to the floor. He took a step back and admired me, just as he did the night in the hotel. My skin burned under the heat of his gaze. Then his eyes narrowed as he zeroed in on my torso.

I stiffened.

He took a step closer and rubbed a circle over my belly, spreading out to my hips then up to my breasts. His hands cupped each breast and lightly massaged. I bit my lip to stop myself from reacting to his hands roaming over my tender breasts.

"You look different," he whispered. His hands continued to work my breasts. "Your tits have grown," he said happily.

"It's the pill." I smiled nervously.

"You're beautiful." His hands moved lower, much lower and two fingers slipped inside. "Christ, Ava."

My head tipped and I groaned. I grabbed hold of his shoulders and widened my legs, giving him better access. Not sure if my hormones were what heightened my pleasure, but I was about to come just by his fingers in less than a minute.

"Jardine," I whispered. "Don't stop."

He chuckled low. "I don't intend to." With two fingers, he pumped in and out, curling, stroking and finding that spot. I arched my back, and tightened my grip on his shoulders. My legs weakened as the pleasure heightened.

When I came, Jardine took my weight, holding me up and kissing my hair.

"Thank you," I whispered.

"I want to say 'my pleasure,' but I think it was all yours." He grinned before releasing me and starting the shower. "You remember the last time we showered together in the hotel?"

I nodded, although not really comprehending his words with sexual bliss consuming my thoughts.

I opened the glass shower door and stepped in under the spray. "What are you getting at?"

Jardine undressed and stepped in beside me, already aroused. His mouth went to my breast, and I groaned when his tongue tickled my nipple. He kissed his way to my neck. "I've had weeks to think and to plan. What we did in the hotel was just like a training session for the real deal."

His hands grabbed my hips and pulled us together. With the shower soaking us, he kissed me, his hands slipping over my skin. Every single spot tingled under his touch. Then he lifted me until I straddled him with my back against the tiles. For a moment, he stared at me, his long lashes tipped with water droplets. I looked into his caramel eyes and could read the love he channelled into me.

"I've never wanted anyone or anything as much as I want you." Then he slipped into me, his eyes slowly closing. I groaned as he filled me, inch by inch, my body spreading around him. His eyes opened and the love was replaced with desire. With each thrust, his movements deepened and quickened until I was calling his name as ecstasy coursed through me. Losing strength, I struggled to hold on to his shoulders.

Jardine's eyes glazed over as he found his release, speaking my name in a whisper. His head tipped forward to rest on my shoulder and his grip tightened around my thighs.

"Ava," he whispered again. "My sundar."

I woke at five with Jardine in a deep sleep next to me.

Not unlike previous nights, I lay awake, thinking. I blamed my erratic hormones. All my fears surfaced at night, and even with Jardine by my side, it wasn't enough to calm my thoughts about the future.

Dark thoughts echoed how our relationship was dominated by sex. Sometimes I wondered why Jardine even loved me. My insecurities pushed further as I considered whether or not he was just using me as someone to screw and get his rocks off. But then I realised he could now get any girl, so if that were the case he'd have dumped his long-distance girlfriend.

The label hung in the air like a dirty smell. How many long-distance relationships of couples my age had I known to work out?

None.

This week might be the last time we'd have sex for many months. Could he last that long without it? And then there was the whole issue of me being pregnant. If I were to tell Jardine, it would have to be this week and it could ruin the fun for the remainder of our time together. I didn't want him leaving confused or angry. I shook my head, trying to clear my head.

"What are you thinking about?" His low, sleepy voice sounded sexy in the dark.

Deep in my own thoughts, I hadn't noticed him stirring. "Us... You.... Me... Life."

"As long as I'm in your life, that's all that matters. Now go to sleep." He rolled over and spooned me.

Spooning always made me feel safe and brave enough to talk without having to see his face. "Why?"

"Why, what?" he muttered.

"Why do you love me?"

He lifted his hand and touched my breast. "Because you have the best tits."

"I'm serious."

He exhaled loudly. "You got all night?"

"Actually, yes."

He pushed up onto one elbow. "You really want to know?" He rubbed the side of his face.

"I do."

His hand touched my cheek. "Because of the freckles on your cheeks. Because you're smart, and that's sexy as hell. You're also sensitive. You think you have flaws, but they're what make you unique and special to me. All I know is if anything great happens to me, you're the first person I want to tell. All I do is think about you. I check my watch and imagine what you're doing at that particular time. And at night, my body actually hurts thinking of you…missing you." He kissed my nose. "You bring out the best in me and that's how I know I love you."

My chest tightened. He loved me as I loved him.

I pushed back a tear and my throat burned, knowing what I had to do. Because I loved Jardine with every fibre of my being. Yet I had no idea how to let go of the person who was, without a doubt, my soul mate.

In one week, Jardine and I made up for our no-sex-for-five-weeks. After his mum and dad arrived home, we planned our private moments, even sneaking quickies in his car.

The intimacy made it difficult for him to leave again. Emotionally, we were more connected than ever and we both struggled to say goodbye.

The morning of Jardine's departure, I drove to the airport to see him off. His father had driven him and then continued on to work at his medical practice. I surprised Jardine by showing up. It was worth getting up early to witness the look on his face. And the way he kissed me, I couldn't blame the other travellers if they assumed we'd been separated for years. Jardine took my hand and led me to seats near his gate. We sat quietly, allowing the closeness of our bodies to speak for us. His flight was announced and Jardine stood slowly.

"Well, this is it."

I pushed up from my seat. "It's time."

So much emotion flowed between us. I rested my head on his chest and closed my eyes, knowing in my heart that this *was* it. There would be no other time to hold him.

His fingers moved under my chin, which he lifted until I met his gaze. "I love you. I always will." He leaned in and kissed me tenderly.

"I hope you understand one day how much I love you."

He jerked away and gave me a quizzical look. "One day? I already know, Ava."

I nodded. "I hope so." He tilted his head, but before he could say anything, I placed my fingers over his mouth. "No goodbyes, okay?"

He stared at me. "Until next time." Then he turned and headed to the gate, stopping to look back at me one last time. I held up my hand to wave and stilled, seeing the tears in his eyes.

My heart split in two for him—and myself—knowing what I had to do.

For the next two weeks, I kept myself busy, trying not to think about the rapidly approaching day when I'd be saying goodbye to Jardine. Every part of me hurt when I thought about never seeing him again. It was a cowardly act to break up with him and then leave for vacation the next day. But when I thought about my options, it was the only one that made sense. I needed to put as much distance between us as possible so he couldn't convince me to change my mind. Jardine had his ways of persuading me, and more than likely I'd crumble.

This year would undoubtedly go down as the worst Christmas ever.

After spending the day shopping with Cleo, we exchanged our Christmas gifts since I was leaving for St. Louis in the morning.

"Are you sure you know what you're doing?" she asked for the tenth time today.

"No. But I have to. There's no other way."

"He loves you, Ava."

"I'm doing this for him. I don't want Jardine to choose me and give up his dream. In twenty years time if we have a fight, I don't want him bringing up that he gave up his cricket dream because I was pregnant. And I guarantee it will divide him and his father. What sort of a person would do that to someone they love?"

Cleo closed her eyes and opened them again. "I know you think you're doing the right thing, but it's going to crush you both."

I gave her a reassuring smile. "I have you and Oliver to help get me through it. And soon I'll have a baby. It won't be about me anymore."

"So you're giving up your life and dreams so Jardine can have his?"

"Yes."

Cleo pulled me into a hug. "I'll be here if you want to talk, okay?"

"Okay."

I placed Jardine's gift on the seat but didn't make it home before Cleo called my phone. I pulled over and took her call.

"Our school results arrived!" she screamed into the phone.

"Serious? What did you get?

"Ninety-six. Enough to get into Nutrition," she sung.

"Congratulations," I said. "I'm truly happy for you."

"Are you home yet?"

"No."

"Well, hurry up."

"It won't matter what score I receive. My plans have changed. My life has changed. No more university."

"But you wanted it so bad."

"I wanted to study with Jardine," I corrected. "It's not the same."

Fifteen minutes later, I arrived home. My universe had shifted and I no longer felt anxious or cared about my results. That is, until I opened the envelope and pulled out a certificate marked with a score of ninety-seven out of one hundred. The walls that I'd carefully constructed since making my decision crumbled upon reading my score. Realising I too could have found my dream and knowing it was no longer a possibility, I fell to the ground on my knees.

CHAPTER 13

Jardine arrived at my house after dinner. As soon as I opened the door, I caught a glimpse of him in a white shirt and khaki shorts before he pulled me into his arms. Like every other time, my whole body softened, welcoming his embrace.

After breaking down this afternoon, I couldn't allow my walls to crumble so easily again. I stiffened in his arms and he released me.

"What is it?" A concerned look crossed his face.

I decided to come right out and say it. "I can't see you anymore."

"What?" His brow creased to a V. "What are you talking about?"

"Every time you go away, it hurts. I'm not cut out for a long-distance relationship."

His lips parted. "For God-sake Ava, please. It's temporary."

"Temporary? Come on, Jardine. You can play cricket into your thirties. It's not the life I want. Every time you leave, it destroys me all over again."

"What are you asking? For me to give it up for you? 'Cause if that's what you want, then I will." He grabbed my hand and squeezed it.

I moved away from the door and closed it, making sure my parents couldn't hear. "No. I don't want you to give it up for me. That's my point. I want you to follow your dream. But I can't stand by and watch you get yours and not find my own."

His gaze lowered and his thumb made little circles on my wrist. "We can do both." His gaze lifted. "Did you receive your score?"

I nodded. "Ninety-seven." The words rolled easily off my tongue, although they held no emotion because there was no dream.

He pulled me into his chest and hugged me. "I knew you could do it."

I relaxed for a moment and absorbed the love flowing from him. I had Jardine to thank that I did so well. He grabbed both my shoulders and stepped back. "You'll accept an offer to get into med school, right?"

I shook my head. "No. I've changed my mind."

He narrowed his eyes. "You always wanted to."

"No. I always wanted to do it with you. And I assume you're not?"

He shook his head slowly. Something crossed his face and I could tell he was processing my words.

I crossed my arms over my chest. "What's your score?"

"Ninety-nine," he said warily.

"Congratulations. You could basically study anything."

He shrugged his shoulders. "Maybe," he said slowly and in a soft voice.

I could sense him feeling some guilt and I never wanted him to. "But you're not... because of cricket." It was a statement more than a question.

His lips pressed into a thin line. "Ava, please don't do this. I know you. This is not you."

"Jardine, I can't see us going any other way but downhill from here. I love you, but you need to follow your dreams and grow as a person…and I need to do the same. One day our worlds may be different and we'll be ready to get back together. Until then, we need to find ourselves without always needing the other in our lives." My hands trembled as my brain registered I was about to cut off my life support.

Jardine gaped at me. "What did I do to you? Please tell me and I'll fix it." His eyes filled with tears and my heart clenched, wanting to take him back in my arms.

I rolled my lips inward and shut my eyes, trying to gather the courage to go on. When I opened my eyes, my chest tightened seeing the tears staining his cheeks. "I'm doing this for you, Jardine. I'm setting you free so you can live your dream. Grow as a new person and be happy." My lips quivered and I didn't sound as sincere as I'd hoped.

Jardine shook his head. "No." He turned away and walked a few steps, stopped, then came back to me. He pulled out a box from his pocket. His Adam's apple bobbed. "I bought you this for Christmas." His voice quivered.

I took the navy velvet box from his grip and opened it with shaky fingers. Jardine watched me open the lid to reveal a gold locket. On the front, our initials were engraved.

J. K.
&
A. W.

A small sob escaped me.

"Here, allow me." Jardine took the box from my trembling hands and looped the gold chain around my neck.

I glanced down at the locket hanging low on my chest. His hands lingered on my skin. "It opens." He forced a smile. "I'll show you." He unclipped it and the locket opened to a photo of the two of us smiling and very much in love.

It broke me.

My knees gave way and Jardine caught me. "Why are you doing this?"

I cried into his chest. "For you."

"I don't want you to do it for me. Tell me the real reason," he croaked.

My hands went around his back, slipped under his T-shirt and felt his strong muscles beneath my fingertips. "One day I hope you understand."

One day I hoped to forgive myself.

He grabbed my shoulders and stepped away. "You're seriously going to break up with me? Tonight?"

"Yes...you have no idea how hard this is."

He gave a sarcastic laugh and let go of me. I stumbled back. "Wait. I have something for you." I rushed inside and grabbed his present from the table in the hall. When I stepped back out, all of the air caught in my throat at the sight of his splotchy face. I held out the present. "Merry Christmas." His eyes narrowed and his arms remained slack at his side. "Please, Jardine."

He took the present from me and ripped at the paper forcefully. He held up the grey T-shirt with a multi-coloured giant *A* on the front. It was from my favourite brand, Astranged Clothing.

"Thank you," he murmured, studying it. "I like it." Then Jardine tucked the T-Shirt under his arm as he pulled the photo frame from the box. I'd selected a photo that Cleo had taken of us, one where I was standing behind Jardine with my arms around him, looking over his shoulder at him while his face was tilted toward me. We were laughing and staring into each other's eyes. "Is this some kind of sick joke?" he whispered as he studied the photo.

"No. I have the same photo in a similar mirrored frame next to my bed. You'll always be a part of me," I said in a softer voice. "I'll always love you."

His gaze lifted and his expression darkened. "But not enough to stay with me?"

My whole body trembled as I fought my heart, which wanted me to renounce my decision. My gaze dipped to the ground and I shook my head.

"Bhaad mein jaa!" Jardine turned and threw the frame like a Frisbee at the gum tree near the path. The glass smashed as it fell to the ground.

I inhaled a sharp breath and took a step back, closer to the door.

Jardine spun around. "In case you're wondering, I said, '*go to hell.*'"

"Goodbye, Jardine." Tears streamed down my cheeks. I opened the door but before I shut it, I caught a glimpse of his back as he stormed away.

My head rested against the door as I waited to hear his car take off. Once I knew he was truly gone, I went outside to pick up the frame. My throat burned with emotion when I realised he'd collected the shattered frame and photo before he left.

I placed one hand on my tummy and stared out to the street, watching the taillights of Jardine's car as they disappeared. "I know you will always love me, Jardine. And that will have to be enough."

The following morning at the airport, I stared at the message on my phone from Jardine, reading it one more time before switching to airplane mode.

I don't know why you're doing this, but I'll give you some space. Go away and think about it. But I intend to call you when you get home. I love you, Ava, and I'm not giving up that easily.

I pressed a finger to my eye to stop a tear from escaping. Last night my parents grilled me about Jardine when I came back inside, and I didn't want more questions today. I had other things to worry about, like trying to determine the ideal time to tell them I was pregnant. I could only hope that they understood my reasons for wanting to raise *my* baby alone.

From the top of the Gateway Arch, I peered out through tiny windows to the city of St. Louis and reflected on my future. Being here inside a monumental structure gave me hope. I'd listened to employees working the elevator and to recordings as we rode to the top. The one thing that stuck in my mind was how the arch signified a new purpose, linking the heritage of yesteryear with the richer future of tomorrow. It typified the pioneer fighting spirit, and I likened it to the baby, my reason to strive for a better life and myself.

After gazing at the city and identifying places like the Cardinals' home field, I moved to the other side and looked down upon the Mississippi River. Tomorrow we'd fly to New York for Christmas and New Year's, and I already knew what to wish for when the big ball dropped.

"Ava, are you ready?" I turned to my dad to see his head inclined to the elevator door.

I bit my lip. "Sure."

He held out his arm. "Are you feeling okay?"

I smiled. "Yes, Dad." Since telling my parents about my baby yesterday, my father wouldn't stop fussing. At first, the disappointment in his expression had upset me, but he quickly recovered and mentioned how I'd caught him by surprise. Mum had remained quiet, only saying a few things. When the shock eventually wore off, I expected her to be happier...or at least accept my decision. I'd already made a mental plan of how I was going to work and be independent.

Last night held more surprises with Dad announcing he intended to accept a promotion on the East Coast of Australia after Christmas. He'd withheld the information from me, not wanting to upset me over the holidays, and because they assumed I'd refuse to leave Jardine.

I sighed at the thought of the irony.

"I've thought of baby names," I said.

Dad's hand went to my back as he led me away from the crowd. "Really? I'd like to hear them."

"Well, I think Louis if it's a boy and Missy for a girl." Dad ran a hand over his dark hair. "Come on, think about it," I joked. "The city and the river..."

"Oh." *Men just didn't get it.*

"Being here signifies a new beginning and a better future. To me, my baby represents a new life and a new dream. The names will remind me of this Christmas, our family holiday and hope."

Dad patted my back. "I think they're good names, Ava. You're a courageous young lady, and I've always said you can do anything you set your mind to."

Uncertainty rolled over me, thinking about starting a new life in a new town. As much as it offered the hope of new beginnings, it saddened me to be leaving my two best friends, knowing how much they've supported me. At least the East Coast was a great holiday destination for them to come visit.

I glanced down to my wrist, my finger tracing along the words *Que sera* that would forever be written there.

What will be, will be.

No matter what the future held, Jardine would always remain in my heart. Thankfully, he'd also stay with me forever in the form of his unborn child, who was growing inside of me. I'd never forget him and hoped he would remember our good times.

Although there was a part of me that feared what would happen the next time we'd see each other and the fallout if he ever found out. My stomach tightened, but then I reassured myself it would be years—if ever—since I'd agreed to move interstate with my family for my father's new job. A list of explanations rushed into my head. None of them, however, were the truth. Jardine would hate me if he ever discovered the truth. So I hoped he'd eventually forget about me and never find out.

I'd made a decision to give him the life he'd dreamed about.

My decision offered the hope of new beginnings for everyone.

CHAPTER 14

Six weeks later…

My parents' new home on the East Coast of Australia was a little piece of paradise.

A paradise to them. A place of new beginnings for me.

It was home, for now…

My parents thought Terrigal was the ideal place to retire, and for me to raise a baby.

A safe haven.

A stranger to the locals who welcomed us without question.

Everything felt right.

Yet this piece of heaven was missing something integral, a piece of my heart that could never be replaced. I inhaled a deep breath and looked out to the ocean lapping the shore, and concentrated on pushing the sensation to a place where all hurt and emotion were locked away.

I promised myself not to keep going around in circles. Promised myself, I would move on and do what was best for my baby, and me. It would be just the two of us, so I had to stop thinking *what if…*

I walked back inside and pulled out my laptop. Before resending my resume to the local businesses, a reply in my inbox caught my attention.

An interview at a café only a short walk from home. Sweeping up my laptop, I found Mum in the kitchen.

"I have an interview at the Hibiscus Café."

Mum turned and wiped her hands on a napkin. "The café down the road by the beach?"

I nodded. "It would be ideal because I could walk. And the hours are seven 'til three, Friday to Monday. No night work."

"On weekends? Well, at least you'll meet plenty of people coming in to dine for breakfast and lunch. It might be a way of making friends." She smiled as though I'd hit the jackpot.

My smile faltered.

New friends would ask questions.

Friends who were entitled to the truth were in Adelaide. Friends who were there for me, and ones I could talk to anytime. Friends who were devastated when I moved away, but understood my reasons, and vowed to help me.

"Maybe," I said before heading to my room to respond to the email.

A week later I had worked my first shift and was serving morning coffee on the second day. It was a Saturday and the café was packed. School holidays finished a couple of weeks ago but holiday goers still frequented the coastline. Even I could make out the difference between a local and a tourist.

"Love, do you mind turning up the volume?" The customer nodded toward the television.

"Of course," I said, my heart missing a beat when I came face to face with Jardine, staring down at me from the big screen mounted on the wall.

My parents didn't watch the cricket around me. Dad had *his* own television room, and no one had mentioned Jardine's name for weeks. And now it was like he was in the same damn room as me.

I struggled to breathe. The part of me that missed him—longed for him—wanted him even more. My arms wanted to grow and reach out to touch his image. The logical side of my brain kicked in and stopped my body from turning limp. I inhaled a deep breath and turned up the volume and spun away from the screen.

"The lad has been playing out of his skin every match." The male customer spoke as if I knew to whom he was referring.

"I don't follow the cricket," I said quickly.

"Pity. No better time to be cheering for the Aussies."

Figured why my father had spent more time in *his* room when he wasn't working.

At night I dreamed of what I would do, and what I would say if I ever ran into Jardine again. Of course, there's a fairy tale ending but my real thoughts understood it wasn't possible. So my mind implemented more measures to avoid him, and forget.

After gathering some dirty dishes, I headed for the kitchen. I needed space to breathe normally.

"Got any plans next weekend?" Florence asked when I dumped the dishes on the sink.

She was around my age, and I had warmed to her since we worked the same shifts.

"Only hanging out here."

She grinned. "There's this wicked annual music festival."

I had seen the posters around town.

"You in?"

"Sure."

She pushed blonde wavy strands behind her ear. "Cool. I'll send you the deets later."

Florence had managed to shift my thoughts away from Jardine by introducing a new problem to worry about. My bump was obvious in anything tight, so I needed to find a dress that was hip and a loose fit.

But how was I going to explain myself to my new friends when I said no to alcohol at a music festival?

Cue the new, weird girl.

In the past when I felt this way I messaged Cleo. She knew the right things to say. I'm so proud of her studying a physiotherapy degree at an Adelaide University. Took us all by surprise considering she was contemplating nutrition and health sciences. I disappeared to the restrooms and sent her a text. If she's not in class or studying then she'd call back.

Before dropping my phone in my pocket it vibrated in my hand.

"Hey you," Cleo said cheerfully.

"Hey," I whispered. "I need some Cleo love."

She laughed. "Always here for you, girl. So a music festival. Not what I was expecting."

"I'm trying to meet friends but I'm not ready for the questions, so I need to buy something that makes me look sexy, and hides my bump."

"You don't need my advice on this chicky. You look amazing in anything. Get something with a low cut top, so it hangs loosely from under your tits."

Nice.

"If you want to cover your bump you have to accentuate your assets."

"Right." I sighed.

"I miss you."

I turned and gazed up at the ceiling. "I miss you, too."

"When are you coming home next?"

"No plans yet. I have no money. And I don't want people to see me. Can you come here in your next uni break?"

"I'll look into it. I'll chat to Oliver and see if he's also keen."

Oliver.

My heart dropped a little more.

"Don't worry, babe, we'll come see you soon enough. I promise."

"Thank you," I whispered.

"Make sure you take a pic of you in that dress and send it to me. You know you really need to get Instagram."

"You know I won't."

"I'm not going to send text message photos to you all the time. Get on it. It's no big deal. You can make up an alias name and have it set so only Oliver and I can see your pics. I want you to follow me, so you can see what I'm up to. And I want to see your baby bump grow. It's a win-win."

I smiled through my sadness. "I'll think about it."

"Good. I'll be waiting for pictures of you in that dress."

Deception is not a sin.

Nor is it a desirable trait and yet lately we are acquainted.

Cleo was right. The sunflower dress fitted snug over my ever-growing breasts before falling above the knee and it had camouflaged my secret.

Giving the material of my cleavage one last tug, I killed the engine and double-checked the address. It matched the text from Florence, so I went through the gate to a path leading to a large, wide wooden door slightly ajar. Two knocks then I heard Florence's voice telling me to come inside.

"Hot as fuck."

I blinked at the guy standing next to her.

"Hey. We were just talking about you. This is River."

River's gaze lowered. The urge to cross my arms was overwhelming but I lifted my chin, determined to be confident. "All good stuff?"

Florence laughed.

"Flo failed to warn me how I'd want to fuck your tits the moment I saw you."

She slapped him. Hard.

"What?" He actually looked surprised.

My face burned.

"His mouth is sluttier than his dick," she said apologetically.

They were only words and yet I wanted to hurl. The thought of anyone else other than Jardine touching me caused my whole body to shudder. "I'm immune to bullshit."

River raised one eyebrow. "We'll see what else you're immune to by the end of the night."

"Back off, River. Ava has a boyfriend." She winked at me.

"He lives in Adelaide," I lied. "We're doing the long-distance thing."

"A dumb fuck for allowing you out of his sight."

Again my cheeks warmed at the way he looked me up and down.

"I mean it," Florence snapped, giving him a dark look before turning to me. She raised her hand holding a Corona. "You up for a beer?"

"I don't drink." I waited for a smart remark, but all I got was a sigh from River.

"What's happening to everyone lately? They're either abstaining from alcohol and soft drugs or turned vegan."

Florence laughed. "I'm only lactose intolerant. I'm still on your party list." She patted him on the back, and only now I noticed her wavy blonde hair was styled straight. It brought out her green eyes against a brown suede halter-top. Her black short skirt paraded long tanned legs.

"Flo-girl you are forever on my list." River's dark eyes looked down at her seductively. Something told me these two were more than friends.

Florence rolled her eyes. "Yeah, yeah. Down that beer your hand's hatching so we can get outta here and snag a good spot near the stage."

CHAPTER 15

Turned out my suspicions were right.

Florence and River had hooked up countless times over the duration of the night. He even tried to kiss me but I had sidestepped his attempt. Party mood or not, I still wasn't relaxed to a casual hook-up or to share a guy with a friend.

I even managed to dance and sing along to some tunes before leaving around ten since I had to get up for work the following day.

Florence didn't show for work, then took another sick day. I should have called her and checked in but didn't in case River and her were at it. I expect to see her at work tomorrow and will then more than likely hear about her week.

Florence I liked, but I didn't feel comfortable around River. So, for now, I followed gut instinct and kept my distance.

When we first arrived in Terrigal, Mum had accompanied me to see an obstetrician. The next appointment was due next week, so I decided to go to a local bookstore and buy *baby* books to acquaint myself. Mum had heard from a friend about 'what to expect' apps so I was also going to download those on my phone.

Until now I was getting on with life, and tried not to be consumed with thoughts about the baby as it led my imagination to Jardine. When I felt the first flutter of movement only days ago, my baby was becoming more of who I am. I knew a part of Jardine was growing inside of me but it was time to differentiate the two in my thoughts.

Time to step up and improve my knowledge on motherhood.

The main street was walking distance so I strolled over hills in search of some reading material. I loved the views and our house near the beach. The hilly landscape not so much when it came to getting around by foot. In the main street I caught my breath, slowing to a stroll before entering the bookshop. I stepped inside and a journal on a gift table caught my attention. It was covered in silver glitter with the words,

LOOK OUTSIDE YOUR DREAM AND AWAKEN THE SECRET

I picked up the book. It was like it could read my mind. I flicked through the blank pages looking for invisible answers. This is where I could share my deepest thoughts, like a friend, getting every emotion out and on to paper. A secret place for my private thoughts. I kept the journal tight in my grasp and wandered between shelved walls. I found a book on the biology of pregnancy, and one on the first few months of a newborn life.

I paid for the books and headed home with an overwhelming urge not so much as to read but to write in my new journal.

"You seem to have recovered well, I said to Florence the following morning.

"Sex can do that to a girl." She turned and gave me her cheeky smile. "Does wonders to vitalise your body. When was the last time you indulged in treating yourself?"

"Indulged in like a spa treatment or are we still on about sex here?"

"Nothing beats sex." Her brows drew together in question. "You need to come out with me on Wednesday when you don't have to work."

I laughed nervously. "Sorry, I'm looking for a second job working at nights. I'm trying to save."

She shot me a sceptical look. "For what?"

My future.

"A new car." The lie sounded convincing. "Have you seen mine?"

Florence nodded.

"And I want to travel."

"We all do. Europe for me. You?"

"India."

The word was out before I even thought about it.

Florence nodded slowly. "And?"

"What do you mean?"

"Has anyone told you your eyes reveal your thoughts?"

I swallowed.

A certain person had told me that on a number of occasions.

"How long have you been here?"

"In Terrigal? Almost two months." The conversation had switched from light to serious, and serious made my stomach tighten. I went about setting tables ready to open the café in fifteen minutes.

"And what have you seen?" she said from behind.

"My parents and I were exploring some areas on weekends before I started working here." It didn't happen every weekend because they were invited to dinner parties. Not my thing even though they insisted I go along since Dad's work acquaintances had adult children. I stopped after dinner number two.

Florence rolled her eyes. "Only the locals know the best spots. Tuesday I'm taking you somewhere special."

"Where?" I asked quickly.

"Flo. Quit jabbering and finish stacking the fridge. We are about to open the doors." Vince, our boss had come through the back door unnoticed.

"It will be a surprise," she whispered.

"I can't make it."

Florence spun around.

"I'm sorry but I remembered I have a doctor's appointment. It's the only commitment I have all week."

The way her eyes softened my face must have portrayed the truth.

"Okay, we can do it Wednesday."

"Cool." I smiled but I turned before she saw the apprehension in my expression.

On Tuesday afternoon Mum went shopping. Alone, and still on a high after my morning appointment, I wanted to capture the emotional high. Bottle it so when I needed a pick-me-up it was there to remind me of the happiness I was capable of feeling. I grabbed my journal and headed outside to sit under a shady tree and breathe in the crisp, salty air.

<u>*3rd March*</u>
18 Weeks

I heard my baby's heartbeat today. It was the most beautiful sound, a constant reminder of love with every beat. All worries dissipated like someone waved a magic wand, and a sense of responsibility overtook everything else.

When Dr Bermingham performed an ultrasound, I kept shaking my head at the tiny foetus, my baby, the size of an artichoke yet fully formed, with all five fingers and toes. Love swelled in that second watching my baby move an arm across his face.

Dr Bermingham asked if I wanted to know the sex. I declined, for now. It will be one surprise I'll look forward to. And yet I referred to my baby as him. It feels more like 'a him.' So until we meet, I'm referring to bubs as Baby Walt. My last name shortened.

Today I kept touching my tummy. I know Baby Walt can sense it. A hand to reach out and connect, and to protect.

A promise I will keep.

<u>*4th March*</u>

Florence gave me three choices: horse riding, abseiling, or lunch at the Bamboo Buddha.

Lunch it was. And I'm glad I didn't bail. The gardens were serene and I tried a vegetarian meal. It was so tranquil. There were times we barely spoke, simply gazed around and took in our surroundings, listened to the sound of streaming water.

Perfect, except I had to go to the restrooms three times. Thanks, Baby Walt, another thing to get used to.

15th March

After feeling renewed yesterday, today was a whole different story.

I went to the newsagent and saw Jardine splashed across the front page of a pile of newspapers. I bought it without thinking twice.

I want to know about his success, but I don't want to be told and reminded of him by anyone else. I want to choose the times, prepare myself, and set my walls in place. I need to know what I'm giving up is worth it, but then I have second thoughts. Hell, sometimes I want to call him and blurt out the truth.

Would he come to me?

I stopped writing a moment to think.

I couldn't do it to him.
Put him in that position.

Now is not the time. He needs more time to follow his dream.

I place the newspaper in my drawer and smile at the image of Jardine before closing it. Should I keep all the newspaper clippings for our baby?

'Our baby'… here I am still hoping one day we will be together again. It might not happen. How many times do I tell myself mine, not ours!

Hell, my head is spinning.

I close the journal and walk outside to breathe in some fresh sea air.

CHAPTER 16

Lying in bed one hand was resting on my stomach, the other scrolling through the news feed on my phone.

Since I deleted Facebook, I'd resorted to retrieving the news in my world news app. As for my close friends I'd have to text them to find out what they were doing.

Tonight I was searching sport. The cricket headlines. I wanted to know and yet I didn't want to know. Tonight I weakened.

His number was in my phone.

His last text was six weeks ago.

Where are you?

I hadn't responded.
The one before read...

Why won't you just tell me where you are?

My thumb tapped before I registered what I was doing.

Congrats. You are doing so well. I'm not surprised though as I never doubted you. I saw your photo in the newspaper. I really am proud. Take care x

As soon as I pressed send my heart skipped a beat.

What the hell was I thinking?

I held my phone for a moment longer before dropping it like hot coal had burned my hand.

It had been eight weeks since the last text. Jardine was in full swing of his cricket tour. He didn't need a distraction, especially by the one who broke his heart.

The silence was torture, waiting.

Would he respond?

Did he care enough to reply? I mean I hadn't replied to his last text so he might ignore mine for a while. The ball was in his court.

Maybe he was in bed sleeping?

Gah! I picked up the phone and stared at the blank screen. Blinking back tears I placed my phone on the bedside table, and rolled over, pushing the pain of giving him up deeper into the dark space in my heart.

It was after one in the morning when my vibrating phone on the wooden table woke me. In the dark I swiped, and squinted at the name on the screen.

Jardine...

"Hello," I croaked.

"Ava." He said it so politely. A matter of fact.

"Jardine."

"Where are you?" His voice was low and hoarse.

"In bed," I whispered.

"You know what I mean." He didn't snap at me. His voice was deep, yearning.

"You know I can't tell you," I said quietly, choking back emotion.

"You can tell me. I'm over this. Tell me where you are. It's not like I can come and see you mid-tour."

"Have you been drinking?"

"The team is out celebrating after our win. We are flying to Sydney tomorrow."

Sydney.

An hour from Terrigal.

"Don't change the subject, Ava."

"Now is not the time Jardine. I only wanted to let you know how proud I am. You're doing amazing."

"Did you watch the game?"

I took in a deep breath. "No."

"So you didn't care enough to watch and yet you're proud? I don't understand."

"It hurts to see you." My throat burned with emotion.

"It hurts to watch me play?" he sounded incredulous. "I'll tell you what hurts. The fact you broke up with me for no reason, and then tell me you miss me and you're proud. How I fought with my parents because we both know my father had something to do with your decision. And then I hear from friends your family moved away and no-one... fucking no-one, will tell me where you went."

"I'm sorry," I whispered.

"No, you're not. What do you really want, Ava? For me to beg?"

"No," I croaked. The lump in my throat grew with more tears.

I heard him inhale. "I miss you."

"I miss you, too." I barely heard my own voice.

"When I finish this tour we can talk. We can sort something out."

I nodded and shut my eyes tight, knowing it wouldn't happen. "Good luck for the rest of the tour."

"I can send you tickets to a game," he added quickly.

"I have a new job... I'm sorry."

"Yeah…" he hesitated. "So am I. Goodnight, Ava."
I only stopped crying when I fell asleep.

I spoke to Jardine last night.

It didn't take long for Cleo to respond to my text.

Shit!! I can't talk I'm in class. What did he say?

I glanced at the time. It was after nine, so hopefully, her lecture would end soon.

The usual. He wanted to know where I am. I sent a text to congratulate him on the team's win. It was stupid, I know. I'm blaming hormones. I want to cry like all the time.

I swiped a tear thinking about our conversation.

I'll call you in an hour. I want to know everything. I think he knows you're on the east coast somewhere. I saw Callum out at The Shores club. He was drunk and come up to me and asked outright where you were. He had heard your family relocated close to Sydney. I said it was none of his business. I think Jardine is still asking around. You know he won't hear anything from Oliver or me.

Thanks x

"Ava," Mum called out. "I'm heading into town to shop for dinner. Any requests? Do you have any cravings?" She smiled as though she understood.

"I'm okay. But can we have pizza for dinner? I really feel like pizza."

Mum laughed. "I remember craving red capsicum but it had to be on pizza. I'll buy up for tomorrow night and we'll have pizza tonight."

"Thanks, Mum." I'm glad she was still going out so I could chat with Cleo without her overhearing. Mum suggested I cut all ties with Jardine. The more I spoke to him the more I'd let slip. And the more I'd weaken. In the beginning I was strong and confident I could do this alone. Now, it was becoming complicated, and the knife that tore up my gut every day reminded me of the love I let go. But if I told him now, and he came to me, it would hurt him to think I didn't trust him enough to tell him. And he would choose me over his career. And it's why I was doing it so he wouldn't pick me.

I headed into my room and opened up my journal. I made dot points of all the reasons I decided not to tell Jardine, and why he needed to follow his dream.

I believed my decision was a selfless act out of love. When I thought about his reaction if he ever found out, I think he'd believe I was selfish. But I couldn't allow my thoughts to eat me up. This was the path I chose, and I have my parents, Cleo and Oliver to help me.

Oliver. How long was it since we spoke?

I had time before Cleo called. I needed to talk to someone to distract me from my own thoughts.

"Here's my favourite girl," Oliver chirped. "I was just thinking of you."

"Really? Are you at work?"

"Yes, and this place hasn't been the same."

I laughed because I knew he was lying. "So what have you been up to since we last chatted?"

"You mean other than work and uni? I'm putting in extra hours here. Dad has promoted me so…"

"You're as boring as me. But congratulations!"

"Ease up."

I laughed. "I wish I was there to help."

"I could use your help. The Christmas casuals have finished and…" I dazed out when a reminder pops up on my phone.

The first of my antenatal classes commence next week and I have to attend alone.

"Ava?"

"Sorry. Something popped up on my phone and I got distracted. It's happening a lot. I can't focus on bloody anything."

"What was it?"

I inhaled a deep breath. "Antenatal classes. I don't want to go."

"Why. It's a chance to meet people and you might become friends since you'll understand what the other is going through."

"Maybe."

"I know that tone. What's bugging you?"

Scratching at my elbow I hesitated before telling him. "I won't have a partner."

"There's more than likely other girls there without partners. Some partners could be working, and I assume some are like you and it's their decision to have the baby alone."

"I don't want questions."

"Hang up."

"What?"

"Not hang up I mean give me a minute."

Oliver rustled something before he spoke again. "When is it?"

"Wednesday night at the hospital."

"I can make it. I was going to Sydney for work anyway. So I'll come via Terrigal, attend the class with you, and fly back the following day."

"Really? You'd do that for me."

Oliver chuckled as though I missed something. "Yes, Ava, I would. *I am.* I'll get something sorted and talk to you tonight."

"Thanks, Oliver! I love you. You're the best."

He chuckled again before hanging up the phone.

A blue ocean against a white sandy beach was a pretty awesome sight when working. The blue and teal shades reminded me of a painting. In between clearing tables and taking orders I'd inhale deeply, and take in the view, clearing my thoughts for a short time. I pinched myself occasionally, not believing I was here, in paradise. It helped get me through the sadness of what and whom I left behind.

The leg of a black aluminium chair scraped the floor, pulling me out of musing to what I should be doing. I continued wiping a table clean and didn't see Florence approach. "I need to tell you something," she whispered.

Glancing up at her I wanted to cringe thinking she was referring to River. An apprehensive look in her eye hinted otherwise.

"We break in fifteen. Meet me outside."

"Sure." I stood and looked around checking if anyone saw us talking. I adjusted my apron, loosening the strings because in a few short days my normal loose clothes weren't cutting it. Pulling at the black material, I managed to position it over my stomach hiding the roundness and being unrestrictive. New customers arrived. While they deliberated over the menu I made their coffees before ducking out back to find Florence.

"Is everything okay?" I walked up to her and placed my arm on her shoulder. I assumed River and her had a fight or even split, if they were even together. Considering I was barely coping with my own relationship bust up, I doubt I'd be able to offer sound advice.

"My visa arrived."

"Visa?"

"Europe, remember? River and I are leaving in two weeks."

"Oh." When she mentioned wanting to travel, I thought it was in conversation.

"Yeah. When it arrived, I thought... *what am I waiting for*?"

"So, you have savings?"

"Not a lot. But we'll pick up some bar work when we arrive."

"And I was starting to like you."

Florence gave me half a smile. "I'll introduce you to some friends before I leave."

Thanks, but I'll be too busy to worry about going out and meeting people."

Florence frowned.

"I'm not as brave as you to take off with limited cash. I'll need to work two jobs to save."

Florence gazed down to my stomach. "And it has nothing to do with the fact you're preggers?"

I stared at her a moment before I found my words. "When did you know?"

"Had my suspicions but damn you're growing girl. I have to go face Vince and tell him I'm outta here. Wait until he replaces me before you give him that news."

"I'm not going to quit. I need the money. Besides I like working here."

Florence touched my arm. "Been here two years. I'll miss the joint, and I'll miss this town. The coast has loads of adventures so don't become a turtle and keep hiding in your shell."

"I get out and see stuff."

Florence folded her arms and gave me one of her looks. "You need to make friends."

"I'm not the party type. And at our age it's what everyone's doing."

"It's what my friends do but some don't. Just don't shut yourself away. I can read you girl and I'm worried about you. Why are you hiding it anyway?"

I sighed. "Because of the father."

"Was he an arse? Did he beat you? Is he looking for you, is it why you moved?"

I raised my hands. "Whoa. No. Definitely not. And kinda."

Her eyebrows arched when her eyes widened. "Really. He's looking for you? You ran?"

The back door swung open when Serena, the chef stepped out. "Vince is asking where you two are. I could hear ya gasbagging through the window."

My heart missed a beat.

Did she hear everything?

"First day off we're meeting up," Florence said.

I nodded. "Sorry," I said as I walked past Serena.

"Only five minutes over our break," Florence said as she walked past Serena.

"He's not payin' ya to chat, Flo," she snapped.

When we were inside Florence whispered, "And she's banging Vince so be careful."

"Got it."

CHAPTER 17

The moment Oliver stepped into the terminal I threw my arms around his neck and leapt into his arms, forcing him to drop his hand luggage.

"Hey my little monkey," he said and kissed my cheek, squeezing his arms around my back to show his affection. "A little heavier from the last time I saw you."

"Shut up."

He chuckled and lowered me to the ground. "So how's life on the east coast?"

"Pretty good. I've made a friend but she's heading overseas on a working visa, so yeah… friend count is back to zero."

He rustled my hair before collecting his case and following me to my car. "These things take time. I know you. Trust is a big thing, so you're not going to make friends with just anyone."

He was right. It was another reason why I didn't let my guard down. Trust had always been a big thing to me.

"I'm all yours for the next three days. I wanted to stay longer but weekends are flat out at Lombardi's."

"I know. I appreciate you coming here. You know that, right?"

When he looked down at me and smiled my whole world lit up. I loved Oliver. I knew he had my back and friends like him were like diamonds. When you have one you treasure it and take measures not to lose it. I looped my arm through his and walked with a spring in my step. It had only been a few months, but Oliver's hair had grown enough to pull up into a man bun. His olive skin was a darker shade, and I guessed he had spent some summer days at the beach doing the things I used to do when I lived in Adelaide.

"Anyways my job is Friday to Monday so it works out well. My time working in Lombardi's has helped with this job. Have to say it's not as nice or upmarket as your restaurant but the view is to die for."

"You'll have to take me there for coffee so I can check it out."

It felt good to share what I've been doing with my life, and show Oliver all the places I enjoy. For the first time I felt like a local, showing a tourist around.

"We'll go home and get you settled. Mum's cooked dinner and then we'll head to the class."

"Sounds good to me. I can't wait to see your parents."

Oliver held my hand as we walked into a room with chairs seated in a half circle. Four couples were already occupying their seats. They appeared to be in their late twenties. I was the only teen. Oliver led me to the opposite side, not letting go of my hand.

A woman with grey-streaked hair entered holding a folder. She greeted the class and sat in a chair facing us all.

"Hi everyone. I'm Karen. I'm hoping you're all here for week one of the birthing class. Shall we start with introductions?" She looked directly at me.

Oliver didn't hesitate. "Hi. I'm lucky enough to be this gorgeous girl's partner. My name is Oliver, and I work at Lombardi's restaurant in Adelaide."

"Adelaide," Karen repeated.

"Yes, a family restaurant. If any of you visit, mention my name and we'll look after you."

Chuckles sounded around the room.

"So you're here with—"

"Ava," Oliver finished.

"But you live in Adelaide?"

"Yeah. I'll be doing the long-distance thing making sure she is okay."

I didn't know whether to hug him or scream. I knew he was protecting me, but it only led to more questions.

"I'm here with my parents and helping Mum relocate for my father's work. It's only temporary. Oliver and I are working it out," I added.

"Welcome to Terrigal, both of you." Karen smiled and moved her attention to the next couple.

I let out a sigh and nudged him. "My partner?" I mouthed. "And how often will my partner be visiting to check on me?"

"As often as you need." He winked, and deep down I knew if ever I needed Oliver he would be by my side in a heartbeat.

I also understood when I next attended the class alone, no one would ask questions, only assume Oliver couldn't make it because of working interstate. It was a small thing but it gave me strength because questions wore me down.

Oliver took my hand and held it as Karen briefed over pregnancy health notes, and the danger signs, and when we should seek medical help. Oliver looked genuinely concerned, as was I, but I couldn't allow myself to dwell on what ifs. My mind was at full capacity. And when the discussion focused on the foetus, and changes at each trimester, Oliver squeezed my hand and mouthed, "Wow."

He looked me in the eye and whispered, "I will be here for both of you."

A promise I knew he would keep.

The following morning I drove Oliver around Terrigal, pointing out my favourite sights in this small coastal town. We finished in the main street for lunch, in a quirky café and gift shop. While waiting for our food we perused the boho gifts, and some crafts that were made by the locals. I came across a poster of Yemaya, her long hair flowing as she sat on a cliff overseeing her ocean and her children. My breath caught, reminding me of Cleo, my friends, and now my own child growing inside of me. I had to have the poster. I wanted to gaze upon it every day, as a statement to be strong and protect my child like Yemaya.

"What have you found?" Oliver asked, peering over my shoulder.

"A poster of Yemaya."

"The deity you and Cleo are into."

"Yep." I looked up and smiled knowing he thought our sacrifices were a little weird.

"She's a protector of her children, like me."

He raised a brow. "You don't need her. You have me."

"I do. I have you both. It's all I need."

Oliver pulled me into an embrace, arms tight around my back, and he kissed the top of my head.

CHAPTER 18

"Hey, sweetie. Do you want to join Mum and me on a quick trip to Sydney tomorrow?"

I placed my fork next to the side plate. I had felt Dad watching me as I toyed with my food.

"No, no. Mum and you go. Have some quality time without me tagging along."

"We would love for you to come," Mum said quickly. If you don't feel safe being here on your own—"

"I never said that."

"I know dear, but you know how we feel about safety first."

I took a deep breath focusing on relaxing my shoulders. My parents haven't changed. Even now, though I'm pregnant and responsible for raising my own child, they still want to protect me and over-parent. As soon as I saved money I intend to move out. It wasn't that I was ungrateful for all they do because I am. "Thank you for the offer, but I'm intending to chill out before work on Friday, and do nothing."

"Come for the drive and relax in the car. I thought we could look for a cot, and pram for the baby," Dad said calmly.

Mum reached across and patted my hand. "We need to start decorating the baby's room."

We.

Right now, I needed Oliver or Cleo to tell me this was not where I would be living forever. "I don't have enough saved at the moment to buy those things."

"Your father does, dear. He wants to do this for you. It will be our gift to the baby." Mum smiled and I really didn't have the heart or the energy to refuse.

I went to bed with thoughts divided.

In the morning I woke with a clearer mind. Appreciating my parents help and not thinking they were taking over. Understood they wanted to support me and hoped they also recognised I needed my independence. Though right now, I relied on them to help me get by and I was grateful.

The road trip took around an hour, and the conversation altered between Dad's work, and what we needed to do to prepare for my baby's arrival. It reiterated how unprepared I actually was, and this shopping venture would tick off many boxes on my list.

Before lunch, Mum and I perused prams and cots in a couple of baby stores while Dad attended a business meeting with a client. He met us for lunch and asked about our morning.

"Prams have changed since we purchased one for Ava, dear."

"How? The purpose hasn't changed." Dad gave Mum a quizzical look.

"The tyre size for instance and some have a bassinet top which can switch with the capsule, and others are for jogging."

"Jogging?" He raised an eyebrow at me.

I giggled. "Yeah, I'll pass on that one."

"So did you buy one?"

"Still deciding." I glanced at Mum and grateful for her opinion. "Though, I have chosen a cot," I said sounding upbeat because I was. It had been a fun day and considering my baby's needs had made it all the more real.

"Did you like the change table that matched the cot?"

I nodded.

"Your father can pay for them and arrange delivery, and we'll pop into the designer shop across the road and pick out a snuggle cot set."

Dad smiled and handed his credit card to me. "Get whatever one you wish."

My heart sank. Was he doing this to get me out of my funk? "I'll find something on sale," I said and smiled.

"Only if it's suitable," Mum responded. "We are allowed to spoil our first grandchild."

"Yes, you are," I directed the comment to both of them. "And thank you."

Dad smiled. "You better go with your mother. Time's ticking."

The designer shop was across the road between a quirky café and a sports shop.

"Perhaps you can call in there after and pick up some new joggers," Mum teased.

"Ha, ha," I said and not laughing. "I'll meet you in five. I'm going to use the restrooms in the café."

Mum nodded in understanding. It was the fourth visit to the restrooms since arriving in Sydney for the day. The café was almost at capacity, and I walked through to the back and noticed I needed a key. Damn.

"May I get a decaf, almond latte to go please," I asked the cashier. After taking my money, I paused. "May I also have a key to the restrooms?"

"Of course." She pointed to a wall where sets of keys hung on hooks.

"Thank you." I darted off in a hurry because 'baby-bladder.'

When I emerged and walked back into the café, I saw Mum standing mid-way at the counter, her back to the entrance and searching for me. Something in her expression wasn't right. "Mum." I waved and she looked my way. "I was out back."

"Yes," she whispered. Her eyes widened.

"I need to grab the coffee I ordered and then we can go."

She grabbed my arm to stop me from stepping around her. "Don't," she whispered.

Why the hell was she whispering?

I peered over her shoulder and froze.

Even from here I knew. At the table near the door, a waiter was taking an order from Jardine. I was as sure as the sun would rise tomorrow it was he. My heart missed a beat. Then it sped up and so did my breathing.

"It's okay," Mum said, and touched my hips in a gentle way to turn my attention to the wall. "Take a seat for a moment. He won't see you over there."

But it wasn't all right. It was far from right. Because opposite him sat a blonde, and in the seconds I watched them, in the seconds I felt the air change, I knew I wasn't going to be okay. Because everything had changed. And nothing will be as I knew it, and in that moment I felt my world shift.

This time Mum didn't whisper. "Sit down. *Now.*"

CHAPTER 19

The blonde had looked at me as though she could sense something was wrong. Her expression must have made Jardine curious to what was happening behind him and he turned. I waved to the window as though I knew someone outside and slid into the red cushioned seat before he fully faced my direction. She turned to look at the door, while I slid across the booth and out of sight.

Mum stared at me, thinking. "Did you notice a back exit?"

"No." I took a deep breath.

What if he wanted to use the restrooms and had to walk past me?

My heart was beating at a canter.

My chest was tight.

My thoughts were torn.

My heart was breaking all over again.

Had he really moved on this quickly?

"What are you doing?" I asked watching Mum fossick through her handbag.

"There." She pulled out a scarf. "I knew I had one in here somewhere. Put this over your head."

I took the scarf and wrapped it over my head, so it flowed down my back covering my hair and part of my forehead. I wanted to peek. Hell, I wanted to watch her body language when she talked to him. More importantly how he responded. If he leant in close or sat back straight against the chair. Because I knew what Jardine would be thinking with one little look. I wanted to walk past and catch a whiff. Bathe in his scent like I used to when I sat close.

With every minute I wanted to run to him. Tell him *our* news. Tell him I still loved him with *all* my heart.

Instead, my brain caught up.

Raising my gaze I met my mother's serious one. One that told me not to try anything stupid. My hand lifted to the engraved heart necklace sitting on my chest. I gathered my thoughts, and tried to calm my racing heart.

Don't panic. Don't do anything rash. Calm yourself.

If Jardine was ordering food we might be stuck here a while. And Dad will be walking past the cafe any minute. I needed to think fast.

"I have an idea," I whispered. One I would regret. I pulled out my phone, and typed.

> *Hey. I'm in Sydney. Heard you were here and wondering if you're free to meet up in the next hour?*

Mum frowned at me. "What are you doing?"

"Trust me on this." I hit send before I changed my mind. "I'm going to lean and have a peep."

Mum slid along the seat level with me to help screen my face. I could see him on his phone. I wanted ever so badly to see his face. But I could see *her* face. Something was up.

He stood.

She stood.

A message flashed across my screen.

Where are you?

We were near Surry Hills, so I needed to think of somewhere further away.

It doesn't matter where. I'm coming now. Just tell me where.

Jardine was saying something to Blondie while walking toward the door. She spoke to the waiter before chasing after him.

It needed to sound realistic.

Bondi Beach

It was around a twenty-minute drive from here.

The waitress appeared at our table. "I'm sorry I didn't see you sitting here. Do you want this to go or make another?"

"It's fine, I'll take it to go."

Mum led the way, checking the street before I followed.

"Are you okay?" she said in a low voice, almost sounding afraid of my answer.

"Not really."

Jardine will be racing to see me, and if he'd been living like me—lost—my soul craving his especially at night, then my text was insensitive and cruel. And yet, I couldn't help feeling a touch relieved he dropped Blondie like a hot coal in the hope of meeting up with me.

I was going to feel even worse after I sent the next text.

One that would break us both.

I'm not at Bondi Beach.

It was a lie.

I thought I could handle seeing you again. But it's futile.

After seeing you today I know I don't have the strength to be as strong as I need to be. I can't do it to either one of us.

We need to get off the merry-go-round. It's not healthy for either one of us to live in hope.

We are finished as a couple so please don't ask where I am. I can tell you we were in the same café by pure circumstance. You didn't see me. It can't happen again because it hurt me to see you. Hurt me to see you with her.

I want to wish you all the luck in the world with your cricket career. Don't ever tell me dreams don't come true. You are living yours.

It's your new life. Give it everything.

I also have a chance at something new.

Please give me the space to do it because I'm giving you freedom to chase yours.

Maybe one day we will see each other again. As friends. Nothing else.

This is the only way to give us a fresh start.

I hope one day you will forgive me.

That one day you will understand.

For Jardine to understand my decision he would need to know the truth.

And the thought scared me so much my fingers trembled.

"It's done." I handed my phone to Mum. "If he messages I want you to delete his reply before I can read it."

Mum took my phone and it buzzed in her hand. She read the message and her gaze darted between mine and the screen. "Maybe it's time you get a new number?"

Tears filled my eyes. My heart cracked a little more.

I could only imagine his response.

If he couldn't contact me then it would be the final hand forcing him to let go.

I had to do it because that's how much I loved him.

EPILOGUE

CAUGHT OUT
Six years later...

I jingled my bracelets up my arm before rinsing the glass in the sink. The tattoo on the inside of my wrist caught my eye. I smiled thinking of the meaning and how Oliver insisted I get the ink.

Carpe Diem.

My new motto.

Seize the day...make the most of the moment...live your life to the fullest...be spontaneous...go for it...

Or, as Oliver had said, "Don't sweat it. You only live once so fuck it, and just do it."

I preferred Oliver's version best.

During the past four years, Oliver had encouraged me to take risks and not feel guilty about being happy. Something I'd struggled with for a while.

Oliver placed a hand on my shoulder. "Ava, can you clear table ten? We have a booking for six guests arriving in five."

I glanced up at him and smiled in my own goofy way. "Sure."

He frowned, and I immediately wanted to tease him. "What?" he asked in a serious voice.

"Nothing." The smirk remained on my lips.

Oliver crossed his arms. "If I'm a joke, I'd like to know why."

This time I laughed. "C'mon lighten up. Isn't that what you always tell me?" I rinsed another glass before glancing sideways to gauge his reaction.

Oliver tilted his head, "I never laugh at you."

Considering we had gone through school together, I snorted thinking of a dozen times when Oliver had laughed at me. Admittedly, most of those occasions were in our late teens and alcohol was to blame. I flicked soapsuds at him. "Liar."

Oliver jumped back. He scanned the main area of the restaurant to check that no one was watching us mess about. When he stepped forward I squeezed water out of the dishcloth and held it up. "Don't come any closer."

He grinned in a way that warmed my heart. I grew up with this guy and I trusted him.

"Are you considering assaulting your boss?"

"You mean, soon to be partner," I corrected.

Oliver stood beside me and wrapped an arm around my shoulder. He kissed my temple and then released me just as quick. "Yeah and I owe you a drink to celebrate your agreement to be my business partner."

My smile stretched almost to my ears. "Well, yes you do. How about we crack open a bottle of Pinot after we close tonight?"

"Deal."

In one swift action, Oliver scooped suds on his finger and wiped them on the tip of my nose. "But until you sign I'm still your boss," he grinned, "so don't forget about table ten."

"Sure thing boss," I said in a mocking tone.

When I finished rinsing the wine glasses after removing them from the dishwasher— because I like my glasses free of detergent residue— I went to table ten and surveyed the mess. Seriously? I scraped the remaining food onto the plates and then neatly stacked plates on one arm, cleaning up the best I could with the free hand.

"You want me to reset the table?" Molly asked as she followed me out back to the kitchen.

I dumped the dishes onto the sink. "That would be great."

Molly was our junior waitress and had worked part-time during the past twelve months while studying fashion design. Since she needed the extra money, and we could rely on her to take additional shifts when the restaurant was booked out. I appreciated her flexibility, as I often needed someone to cover my shifts at short notice.

My life — it is what it is.

I adjusted the leather wristband to reveal the tattoo on my other wrist.

Que Sera.

Since getting this tattoo at eighteen, my life had changed dramatically over the past six years. The tattoo signified much of my life, and moulded me to who I am now, and all because of one person who still owned my heart. I pushed the leather ties down to cover the words. Not to forget, as I'd never forget him or the best gift he'd ever given me, only to stop the hurt that pierced my heart every time I remembered us.

"You're looking beautiful tonight. Got a hot date later?" Piero called out from behind a stainless steel countertop.

"Does Oliver know? Can this new man be trusted?" Dominic waved his knife at me instead of his hands in his usual gesture.

I fisted my hands on hips. "You guys act like my parents." I shook my head. "There is no guy, all right?"

"We notice when our Bella is sprucing up. There must be a man, no?" Dominic waggled his finger at me.

"No guy. I had time before work to apply make-up. Sorry to put you sniffer dogs off your scent."

"I'm not convinced." Piero winked at me, reminding me of Oliver.

Dominic, Oliver's uncle, had worked the past thirty years as a chef, and was one of the best Italian chefs in Adelaide. His son, Piero, also worked as a chef after finishing school, and was trained by his father. Unfortunately, Dominic lacked the bookkeeping and sales skill that Oliver's family possessed. Sadly, their restaurant closed two years ago. When Oliver's father stepped down to allow Oliver take over the reins of the Lombardi family restaurant, he was happy to not only have his relatives work beside him, but also to have renowned chefs join his staff.

Piero and Oliver have the same dark hair, brown eyes, and olive skin. Lombardi traits that are glaringly obvious when you stand the two guys next to each other. Since I returned home to Adelaide from the east coast of Australia, with no family for support, Oliver and his family took me in as one of their own. I don't know what I would have done without them.

I headed out the back door to the staff-only restrooms. I was still riding the wave of excitement at being offered a partnership at Lombardi's restaurant. It baffled me why Oliver didn't offer it to one of his cousins. I wasn't family but I acknowledged Oliver and I were more than friends. The way he took care of Louis and me, we really were more like family. I couldn't say he acted like a husband because there was no sex. Then again he's not like a brother either, because we did have sex...once. I groaned at that awkward memory. A best friend with benefits was a big mistake. At least we could say that we knew each other well, and we both agreed it wasn't going to be that way between us. We cared for each other too much to ruin it with sex, even though it was a time in my life when I needed physical love.

Oliver understood.

He also understood that I'd given my heart away when I was eighteen, and never recovered. I would never be the same after breaking up with my boyfriend, when I found out I was pregnant, so he could keep his dream of touring the world with the Australian cricket team. Said boyfriend never knew about the baby. I simply disappeared.

Even though I didn't say his name, it still hurt. I sucked in a deep breath and pushed out the memory. My fingers went to the locket around my neck. The last gift he had given me before I told him to leave. I touched the locket and stared at our initials engraved on the front.

A.W. & J.K.

Ava Walters and Jardine Kumble.

My stomach tightened as it always did when I remembered the night he gave me the locket. I glanced down at the thick leather wristband that covered the tattoo I shared with Jardine. I wore the leather every day in a hopeless attempt to block him from my thoughts. Then I shifted my gaze to my other wrist and thought about Oliver, and everything he had done for me.

"Come on Ava. Get your shit together. Oliver has offered an opportunity of a lifetime so...carpe diem," I murmured.

As I washed my hands, I glanced at my reflection in the glass above the basin. I checked my eyes—no black wayward lines—and my dark hair remained in a messy bun on my head, although it was tidier than usual. Admittedly, I looked kind of okay tonight.

When I walked through the kitchen, Piero called out to me, "Boss wants to talk to you before you wait on the new guests."

I waved my hand at Piero and continued through to the dining area. I'd heard all of Oliver's speeches before, and knew how to handle the posh guests that dined here often. Surely the guests that had arrived weren't complaining about waiting for service...I didn't spend that much time in the restroom. Besides Molly would cover my tables if needed.

Striding past the reservation desk I grabbed my electronic Waiter Pad. "Got it," I said, as I passed Oliver who was tapping madly on his iPhone. Strange. Oliver rarely used his iPhone at work.

"Ava, wait!" he called out.

I turned, surprised by what I saw. Concern, worry, and a touch of anger in his expression confused me. If Oliver didn't think I was capable, or trusted me with important guests, why the hell did he ask me to be his partner?

"I got this," I mouthed. He ignored me and strode around the desk towards me. Determined to prove myself and annoyed that he was acting this way, I continued to table ten and stopped. I looked at the first gentleman sitting closest to me. "Sorry to keep you all waiting. Welcome to Lombardi's Restaurant. Can I get you something to drink?"

"Our drinks have been taken care of. May we order starters?"

"Sure." Out the corner of my eye I noticed Oliver stop, and watch me. The guests were not as posh as I expected so his attitude threw me. Maybe I missed something? My gaze swept around the table. Two blonde girls were dressed in sexy black numbers, wearing a hell of a lot of make-up. Oliver's reaction didn't add up.

The guy, sitting beside the blonde, had his body angled away from me, with one arm in a sling. He turned slowly.

"Ava," the man whom I shared the other tattoo with, breathed.

My fingers gripped the pad upon hearing the voice that had haunted me for years. My gaze locked with his, then all the air whooshed out of me as a wrecking ball smashed into my chest.

I couldn't speak. My hands fell limply to my sides. All I could do was stare. Jardine had become more beautiful, if that were even possible. His hair was darker—and shorter—his jaw had a strong angle and his mocha skin gleamed under the restaurant's dim lights. A caramel haze veiled me, as his gaze bore into mine.

Oh God, oh...

The room tilted and then out of nowhere a warm arm wrapped around my shoulder and pulled me close to a familiar body. Oliver's lips pressed to my ear. "I'm sorry, I tried to warn you. Go out back. I'll take it from here."

I nodded, my gaze still caught under Jardine's intense expression. His eyes narrowed and he released me, his gaze lifting to meet Oliver. "You seem to have everything under control."

His bitter tone brought me back to where I was, and what I should be doing.

"I do," Oliver replied in a low confident voice. "But my partner needs to attend to matters out back. Please excuse her. Molly will be here soon to take your order."

Breathe, I told myself as Oliver led me away, my legs trying to remember how to walk. Then a female voice said the words I'd only ever imagined in my nightmares.

"Do you know that waitress, darling?"

Jardine and Ava's story continues in the sequel CAUGHT OUT

ACKNOWLEDGMENTS

First and foremost to my husband, Lynden. Without your encouragement, love and support, my books would still be sitting on the computer. You are my rock.

To my four beautiful daughters, Jamie-Lee, Shauni, Ashleigh, and Demi, who helped with character names, plot, and provided constant inspiration. Also to Cameron, Charlie and Cruise, who answered my questions on sport. Charlie, thank you for loving cricket!

To my wonderful parents, Pam and Vic Hockley, and sister Vickie and her family, for believing in me and helping in any way possible.

A big shout-out to my biggest fans: Mum, Deanne and Helen, Dayna, and Al, for reading Jardine in its raw stage, and believing in me. I thank you from the bottom of my heart, as your words of praise mean so much to me.

To Jen Naumann, thank you for your encouragement, words of wisdom and late night chats despite the time difference between our countries. Thousands of miles across the ocean and no matter how busy you are you still find time to help. I'm excited for the day we will meet.

To my Adelaide author buddies Carla Caruso, Lilliana Rose, Maggie Mundy, Kim and Kaylene Osborn. Thank you for our coffee dates. We have fun while discussing writing craft. Thank you for helping and inspiring me. You're my writing family and I love you!

A big thank you to my Leesa's Lovelies Facebook Team. You're the best!

Thank you to Archana Desai for helping me with the Hindi terms.

To Kim Sutton, and Blogging for the Love of Authors. I'm so, so grateful for your support, and love in getting my books out in the world. Your love for books and authors truly shines bright. And for helping me select the right cover for my books. We work great as a team.

A special shout out to Kaylene Osborn of Swish Design and Editing. Thank you for making my books beautiful! I'm so appreciative for you being available to help me whenever I message in a panic. A true friend, and mentor. <3

Check these links for more books from
Author LEESA BOW.

NEWSLETTER

Want to see what's next?
Sign up for my Newsletter.
http://eepurl.com/56B_9

GOODREADS

Add my books to your TBR list
on my Goodreads profile.

AMAZON

Click to buy my books from my Amazon profile.

WEBSITE

https://www.leesabow.com/

TWITTER

Jardine

https://twitter.com/LeesaBow

INSTAGRAM
@leesabowauthor

EMAIL
leesa.j.bow@gmail.com

FACEBOOK
https://www.facebook.com/Leesabowromance

LEESA BOW

Leesa Bow loves to read and write spicy romance. She spends her spare time with her family, catching up with girlfriends in cafes, or taking long walks along the beautiful, southern beaches of Adelaide, Australia.

Leesa's love of sport has inspired her to write stories about hot Aussie heroes and the strong women they fall in love with.